MISSING MIA

PJ FIALA

COPYRIGHT

Printed in the United States of America

First published 2022

Fiala, PJ

MISSING MIA / PJ Fiala

p. cm.

1. Romance—Fiction. 2. Romance—Suspense. 3. Romance - Military

I. Title – MISSING MIA

Paperback ISBN: 978-1-942618-66-9

FRONT MATTER

Let's stay in contact, join my newsletter so I can let you know about new releases, sales, promotions and more. https://www.subscribepage.com/pjfialafm

DEDICATION

I've had so many wonderful people come into my life and I want you all to know how much I appreciate it. From each and every reader who takes time out of their days to read my stories and leave reviews, thank you.

My beautiful, smart and fun Road Queens, who play games with me, post fun memes, keep the conversation rolling and help me create these captivating characters, places, businesses and more. Thank you ladies for your ideas, support and love. The following characters and places were created by:

Mia Gregory - Nicky Ortiz (Mia) Shelby Gregory (Gregory)
Mia's friend Andrea - Theresa Solecito Natole
Mia's Aunt Rebecca - Judy Hamilton
Mia's Uncle David Hamilton - Kim Kurtz
Mia's Brother - Ashton Stewart - Kerry Harteker
Mia's editor - Gabriel Francisco - Dana Zamora
Caiden Marx - Laura Rachwalik (Caiden) Margaret Mathias Park (Marx);
Dominick Nelson - Melissa Hultz

Smoky Ridge - Debbie Zsidai
Police Chief Joshua David - Lisa Gibbs
District Attorney Kole Gray - Kelley Todd Perrin
The Summit - Marlene Davis
Goldie's Diner - Kristi Hombs Kopydlowski
Benedict's Cafe And Coffee House - Terra Opening
Nadia Petrov- Kim Kurtz
Skinner66 - Karen Cranford LeBeau
Jasper Mitchell - April Shindlebower Brown
Tannon Marcel - Arlene Miklovic
Dirty Duds - Deb Jones Diem
Double Dippin' - Julie McAlister

Last but not least, my family for the love and sacrifices they have made and continue to make to help me achieve this dream, especially my husband and best friend, Gene. Words can never express how much you mean to me. To our veterans and current serving members of our armed forces, police and fire departments, thank you ladies and gentlemen for your hard work and sacrifices; it's with gratitude and thankfulness that I mention you in this forward.

BLURB

A cyber operative searching for answers.
A reporter with a secret identity.
The story of a lifetime that brings them face-to-face.

Caiden Marx has had to put his personal sorrows on the back-burner since his high school sweetheart was believed to be killed by a drug dealer. The experience shaped him as a man, making him overly protective of women and children. That's why he's so incredible as a RAPTOR operative. But while on a mission in Las Vegas, Caiden sees a ghost, who seems very much alive.

Mia Gregory has lived on the run most of her life. Witnessing the murder of her mother at a young age taught her to stay hidden or die. As an adult, she's vowed to ferret out those who bring harm to women and children, and shine a bright light on them. She never allowed herself to dream of finding her long-lost love, or her brother in the same year.

Can Mia put her fear aside and allow Caiden to help her? Will they find love once again?

GLOSSARY

Read the prequel to RAPTOR - RAPTOR Rising here. https://www.pjfiala.com/books/RR-BF

A Note from Emersyn Copeland:

Founder of RAPTOR (Revenge And Protect Team Operation Recovery).

I was wounded when my convoy hit an IED and retrained through OLA (Operation Live Again) to perform useful services for the military; mainly locating missing children. Empowered by the work but frustrated by governmental limitations, I contacted my father Dane Copeland and my Uncle Gaige Vickers, GHOST's leader, to form a covert group not restricted by governmental regulations, consisting of highly trained post military men and women with injuries and disabilities. Our offices are housed on the GHOST compound. I divided RAPTOR into three teams of expertly trained individuals who were selected for their specific abilities. Let me introduce you to the Teams.

Team Alpha: Recon and Recovery:

Diego Josephs: Former Army Recon expert. Friend of GHOST Josh Masters. Recent retraining for OLR (Operation Live Again). Demonstrative and possessive, he is a team player battling PTSD.

Ted: Diego's Therapy and service dog. A mix of black lab and Newfoundland.

Donovan "Van" Keach aka the "Reformer": Completed OLR with Emersyn. Blinded in his left eye during a military operation. Out spoken, opinionated, daredevil with a strong belief in service and a mission for justice no matter the risk.

Charlesia "Charly" Sampson: A friend of Emersyn's Aunt Sophie. Medically discharged after she lost her left arm at the elbow during a mission in Afghanistan. Tough adaptable, independent sarcastic, and determined but self-conscious of her appearance. Excels in disarming and getting people to trust her and ferreting out information.

Team Bravo: Cyber Intelligence:

Piper Dillon: Attractive and energetic with a ready smile but all business. Expert computer hacker, communications device expert and internet guru.

Caiden Marx: Strong and independent, Caiden suffered lung damage while serving due to an explosion and fire. He struggles to breathe and can't take on energetic tasks but excels on Team Bravo and has unique hacker abilities.

Deacon Smythe: Deacon has a ready smile and is always happy but takes his job seriously. He's an expert on computers and communications.

Team Charlie, Special Ops:

Falcon Montgomery: Son of Ford Montgomery, a GHOST team member, Falcon lost hearing in his right ear. Growing up with Ford, Falcon is a natural in special ops, and willing to go the extra mile to get the job done.

Creed Rowan: Former SEAL, well rounded in terms of skill, Creed's specialties are explosives and swimming. His abilities take him places others don't dare go.

Emersyn Copeland: Daughter of GHOST founder, Dane Copeland and niece to current GHOST owner, Gaige Vickers, Emersyn's strengths are in business and extracting her staff member's special talents. But, she's equally good at ferreting out suspects' deep dark secrets.

House Staff:

Sheldon Daniels, Cook: Former military, Marine. Friend of GHOST's house keeper and cook Mrs. James. Demands order in his kitchen, punctuality and the keeper of all secrets, bonus he's a damned good cook.

Shioban O'Hearn, Housekeeper: Sassy mid- thirties housekeeper. Loves the thrill of working with badasses, but doesn't let herself get walked on.

1

Caiden listened as Royce's phone rang. He knew this was irritating, after all, Royce and Piper were on their honeymoon, but Caiden just had to find her. Mia. He'd always wondered what happened to her. He'd always dreamed of what she'd look like today and if he'd recognize her if he found her. The answer was yes. The instant he saw her picture on Royce's phone, he knew her.

"Hey Caiden."

"Royce, the newspaper won't give me any information on Mia and they won't let me in the building further than the front desk. Can you give me anything on her?"

"I told you when Piper and I get home, I'll set up a meeting with the both of you."

"That isn't for another week. I don't have a week here Royce. Do a guy a favor."

Royce chuckled on the other end of the phone and Caiden felt some relief. He didn't mean to be a pest, but he did want to find Mia.

"I can give her a call and tell her you're looking to meet her."

"No. I don't want to freak her out. Where does she hang out?"

"I don't know. We aren't that close Caiden. She's a reporter. I have her work number. That's it. The only other thing I know about her is that she used to work at The Summit. It's a casino down on the old strip, just off of Fremont Street. Maybe someone down there knows something about her."

"Thanks, I'll give it a shot."

Caiden hung up the phone and grabbed a light jacket. It was getting to be evening in Las Vegas and even though it was a large city now, they were still in the desert. It could get downright cold at night.

He pulled up the directions to The Summit on his phone, then set out to take a walk. It would be at least a four-mile hike, but he needed to get out and exercise his lungs. Since they'd been damaged in an explosion in Afghanistan, he needed to exercise them at a minimum of five days per week or they weakened, and he struggled to breathe.

The hotel was a maze of hallways and coves, but they'd been here a couple of weeks now and he'd navigated them well. The cigarette smoke in the casino area always made him cough and feel sick, so he'd practiced holding his breath as long as he could, then he'd put his arm over his mouth to breathe in, then hold his breath the rest of the way out of the casino. They really should have a way to walk out of the casino without having to walk past the smoking area, but then the casino would likely lose money as the casual passer-by wouldn't drop in extra coins.

Stepping out of the casino and taking a deep cleansing breath, at least as deep as he could go without coughing, was like a drowning man taking in air again. He took several breaths as he stood on the sidewalk before beginning his journey. Once he knew he had replenished the air in his lungs, he turned to the left and began walking to the downtown area. Walking on the strip was more of a maze than the hotel hallways. Out here you had to go up and down escalators, around buildings, under walkways--it was, at best, a hodge-podge of buildings that had added on, expanded, or built onto and around existing structures. It would be easy to get turned around in this town.

Caiden walked to the end of the strip and began his journey to the downtown area. Flashes of Mia, the last time he'd seen her, filled his mind. She was a beautiful young woman with the brownest eyes and long, dark, shiny hair. She was fresh-faced and gorgeous with very little makeup on. He'd taken her to homecoming their junior year of high school back in West Virginia, and that had been the first time he'd seen her with makeup on. He couldn't look away. He'd always thought she was beautiful, but that night, she'd looked grown-up, mature, and incredibly sexy. It was also the first night they'd had sex and he'd relived that night over and over again in his mind. The way his heart raced when she'd walked in the living room at her mom's house. His throat had dried, and he felt embarrassed at not being able to say anything. Mia's mom had said, "See, I told you, you look gorgeous. Caiden is speechless."

Not three weeks later, Mia was gone, and her mom was dead.

Caiden took a drink from his water bottle, then tucked it back into his pocket and continued his walk. Sections of this part of the street were cut out; the sidewalk removed for construction left the sections muddy and filled with ruts. He looked up ahead as the sun began to set and saw a rat run from an old boarded-up building.

He'd avoid that building by crossing the street at the intersection, but it looked like there were others up ahead.

Finally, making it to The Summit, Caiden took a deep breath and held it as he entered. Typical that you'd walk right into the gambling area from the street, that's how they captured gamblers. He held his breath as he walked on the brightly patterned carpeting, the cacophony of bells ringing and the constant chimes, chirps, and sounds of the machines ridding people of their money. He followed the signs to the bar as he went. His fingers wrapped around the inhaler in his pocket as he neared the end of his held breath. He followed his routine to breathe, shot the inhaler into his lungs once, then continued through to another room, that thankfully was the bar. It was quieter in here, more serene.

A raspy voiced older woman was on the stage singing the standard country songs to a small but rapt audience; the bartender looked to be in his late fifties. Caiden sat on a barstool and waited for the bartender to notice him, then nodded to get his attention.

"What can I get you young man?"

Caiden chuckled. "How about a bourbon."

"You got it."

He watched the bartender pour the golden-brown liquid into a short plain glass then carry it over and set it in front of him. This time when he inhaled, the aroma of an oak distilled bourbon reached his nostrils and he enjoyed it.

He lay a twenty on the bar and the older man walked away to cash him out. When he brought Caiden's change back he made small talk.

"Where you from?"

"Indiana. About fifty miles outside of Indianapolis."

"I've never been there myself."

"It's nice. Small town, easy living."

The older man chuckled, and Caiden took the opportunity to question him. "Have you worked here long?"

He shrugged, "About thirty years."

Nodding, Caiden forged ahead, "Ever work with Mia Gregory?"

"Oh goodness, I sure did. She still stops in from time to time to say hello. Great woman, she's a crack reporter for the *Vegas Herald*. Damn good. Just had a doozie of a story this week about the Sinners. Those assholes."

"Yeah, I read about them. Glad she had a contact and could help to get the word out."

The older man nodded. "Me too."

"How often would you say she comes in?"

"How do you know her?"

"We were friends back in West Virginia when we were in school. I heard she lived here now so I thought I'd look her up and say hi while I'm in town."

The older man nodded and locked eyes with Caiden. Holding his gaze steady, Caiden adopted a nonchalant look that said, business man. Casual. Not really giving a crap. But inside his mind was whirring. His heart was thumping in his chest and his breathing was uneven and it was difficult to take a deep breath.

"You alright? You're breathing is raspy."

"Yeah. I'm a Vet. Lungs were fried in an explosion a few years ago. So, sometimes my breathing isn't smooth and even." He inclined his head toward the casino. "Likely from the cigarette smoke filtering in."

The older man nodded. "Sorry. Thank you for your service."

Caiden nodded but said nothing. After all these years he still didn't know what to say when someone thanked him for serving. He'd served because he wanted to. He loved this country and he wanted to do everything he could to protect it. He was still serving, though in a different vein, and a different group of people entirely. Maybe he should just let Mia go. She hadn't tried touching base with him all these years. Clearly, she didn't think of him as he thought of her.

The bartender cleared his throat, "Eh, I'd say maybe every couple of months Mia stops in to say Hi. Myself, Wendy over there." He pointed to a woman waiting tables across the room. "And Suzie." He pointed to the hostess standing at a podium at the entrance to the lounge area. "All worked here when Mia did. We're as close as you can get in a town like this."

Caiden smiled a soft smile. "It's nice to have co-workers you like and keep in touch with."

"That it is." He wiped the bar down next to Caiden as he chatted. "You won't find her here for a while. She stopped in last week and we had a drink together. Now your best place to touch base is the little cafe on Front street, called Goldie's Diner. Mia has breakfast there a couple times a week."

Could he be so lucky? He wanted to jump up and run out the door and find the café. He wanted to fist pump the air at this good fortune.

But he nodded instead. "Thank you. I'll check it out while I'm in town."

The bartender kept working, but he eyes landed on Caiden several times. He was watching him. Gauging him. And, Caiden had no doubt this man had Mia's phone number. If he were suspicious at all, he'd call her and tell her not to go to Goldie's. So, Caiden continued to sit, nurse his bourbon and watch the folks around him.

The singer took a break and the bar filled up as folks moved around and bellied up to the bar to wait for the next set. Caiden took that time to leave a healthy tip for the bartender, nodded to him and said, "Thank you. Have a great night."

"You too."

Caiden then pulled his inhaler from his pocket, and before hitting the casino where the smoke was thick, took a shot from it, to help expand his lungs. He then took a deep breath and held it as he walked through the casino.

2

Mia scrolled through the comments at the bottom of her story to see what readers were saying about it. There were some haters blaming her for the Sinners' team falling apart. Those were rabid fans of the players who'd been incarcerated or were under investigation, and were mad at their sports idols getting caught being naughty. Ironic that they weren't mad at the players for kidnapping and prostituting young women and children. And there were those who jumped on and posted that as well. All in all, her article had been out for less than a week and so far the comments to the article were nearing the one million mark. She'd never had a story go viral before and the attention this generated was only good to bring light to the trafficking issues in the world.

After reading several comments, she closed the lid on her laptop, and tucked her computer into the carry case for it. She had to go into the office today. Normally she was out in the field finding a story, but today was staff meeting, reporter meeting, and finally one-on-one with her editor about ideas for her next story.

She tucked her white blouse into her navy slacks, adjusted her thin belt, and slipped on her dark-blue-tennis shoes. Then she went to her closet and pulled out her blue pumps for the office, tucked them into her computer case, slipped her cross-body purse over her head, and walked out of her apartment. She was only three blocks off the strip in Las Vegas and it was the perfect location to be able to walk to work or hop on the monorail to make time if she needed to. Today, though, she'd walk. When she went to the office, she stopped at Goldie's Diner for breakfast. Usually because she'd likely miss lunch, or it would be something from the vending machines in the basement of the building. She'd make up for it at supper.

Mia took the elevator to the first floor of her apartment complex. She hardly knew any of the people in the building. They changed so often there wasn't a chance to get to know them. Plus, she worked a lot, and most of the time her hours were so irregular it was difficult to meet up with anyone. She had only made a few connections in all the years she'd lived here in Vegas. Barry, who tended bar, Suzie who was the hostess, and Wendy, who waitressed. She'd met them all when she started working at The Summit. They'd watched over the young girl who didn't seem to have anyone in her life she could count on. They were her mother and father figures. Even they didn't know they were all she had.

She walked on the sidewalk toward Goldie's. The sun was already high in the sky, the air was fresher in the morning than it would be later on today. The sidewalks weren't shoulder-to-shoulder packed with tourists and drunks, but they would be by the time she walked home from the newspaper.

It was going to be a warm day though and she second-guessed her decision not to pull her hair up off her neck. The dark color seemed to absorb the heat from the sun. She could always coil it up and shove a pencil in it later if she needed to.

Opening the door to Goldie's, the delicious aroma of bacon and fresh coffee wrapped around her like a warm hug. Of course she loved eating here. She loved the quaint atmosphere of a small-town cafe nestled right in the middle of a big city. She loved that most tourists were looking for the flashing lights and chrome and glass atmosphere of Las Vegas, while the residents craved something not that at all. She found a table for two at the back corner, which always suited her. She could sit with her back to the wall and see the entire restaurant from her vantage point while hardly being noticed. She'd worried about someone sneaking up on her for half of her life. When she fled her hometown in West Virginia at the age of seventeen she'd at first thought about finding some obscure small town so far off the beaten path that no one would find her. But that felt scarier and offered less protection than getting lost in a big city where most people wore costumes and feathers and masks.

"Hi Mia. What can I get you today, honey?"

"Morning Lucy. I believe I smell bacon, fresh coffee and let's add some crispy- fried hash browns and an egg over easy please."

Lucy laughed. "You got it, sweetie. I'll be right back with your coffee."

Lucy was probably not her real name. Mia had asked a couple of times, but Lucy always responded, "With looks like this, what else would my name be?" Red hair, styled in the signature Lucille Ball upsweep. Red lipstick, creamy white skin, though the years had etched their lines in. She was a pretty woman of a certain age and frankly, if you were going to hide in plain sight, Vegas is where you'd do it.

Mia pulled her phone from her cross-body bag, lay it on the table in front of her and scanned for any new emails that needed to be tended to before she arrived at the office. She saw a news alert about Royce Roman—Off The Market and she smiled as she opened it. The news article from a competitor of hers wrote about the promising, young, handsome quarterback being married at his home in Las Vegas with only family and close friends in attendance. A beautiful picture of Royce and Piper smiling sweetly at each other was embedded in the middle of the article. Mia had been invited but was deeply involved in her article about the trafficking. Royce understood completely. He was so happy she didn't think he cared who was there, except of course Piper.

"May I sit with you?"

The deep male voice startled Mia from her reading. But when she looked up into the blue eyes she'd never forgotten, her mind froze. She stared into his eyes and he stared right back. She tried discerning his mood; his body was tense, his jaw twitched the longer they stared.

She blinked to see if he was real. He was. Real. Caiden Marx stood before her like the ghost of Christmas past.

3

Caiden stared at Mia for what felt like an eternity. He wanted her to tell him yes, he could sit with her. And, regardless of her answer, he was going to sit. But, in case she took off running, he was going to wait for her to agree.

She blinked several times, her lips parted as if she was going to say something, but nothing came out. Then she swallowed and took a deep breath.

"Um, sure." She said it so softly that the noise in the cafe almost drowned her words out. But he heard them.

Slowly pulling the chair from the table, he watched her for signs that she would bolt. She bit her bottom lip and watched him as he sat across from her.

"Honey, I didn't know you were waiting for someone. Can I get you something?"

A red-haired waitress who seemed to know Mia stood waiting for her question to be answered. She wore her hair like Lucille Ball and it was red like hers too.

"Coffee please." He replied.

"No breakfast?"

Caiden looked at Mia, "Are you eating?"

"Yes."

He looked at the redhead and nodded. "I'll have what she's having."

Without writing anything down she nodded and walked away. She was back within a minute with a cup of coffee which she slid in front of him. A fresh pot in her other hand, she topped off Mia's cup then was gone in an instant.

"How did you find me?"

"Royce Roman."

"What? He..."

Caiden held up his hands to stave off what he feared was an angry reply. "To be clear, Royce didn't tell me you were here. Let me rephrase. Royce married my co-worker Piper. I was at Container World rescuing those women you interviewed. When you emailed Royce the article, I happened to be standing next to him and saw your picture. I asked about you. He told me you were Mia Gregory."

"You were at Container World?"

"Yes."

"You're RAPTOR?"

His brows furrowed momentarily then he shook his head. "I'm part of RAPTOR."

"You save women and children." It was a statement not a question.

He watched her process the information he'd just shared, as their waitress brought their food.

Mia picked up her fork and moved her hash browns around on her plate but didn't eat.

"Mia. Where have you been?"

Her eyes, a rich brown that rivaled her coffee, though with russet streaks close to the pupils, snapped up at him. He'd dreamed of these eyes for the past sixteen years.

She shook her head no. He slowly reached his right hand across the table and lay it on her left hand.

"Honey, where have you been? What happened to you?"

When she looked up, tears spilled from her eyes. He reached forward and swiped at them with his thumb.

"Do you want to go somewhere else?"

She nodded. He got their waitress's attention and the concern on her face when she saw Mia crying was immediate. "Honey, here." She pulled a tissue from her pocket and handed it to Mia.

Giving Mia a minute, he said, "We'd like boxes to take our breakfast home please."

"Of course." But before she walked away she waited to make sure Mia was in agreement.

"It's okay Lucy. He's right, we'd like to take our breakfast home." She sniffed delicately.

Caiden chuckled. "I thought she looked like a Lucy."

For the first time Mia smiled.

Lucy returned quickly with two Styrofoam containers and Caiden pulled two twenties from his wallet. "For both of them. Keep the change."

Lucy smiled. "Thank you, handsome."

Caiden began transferring their food into the containers and Mia picked up her phone and placed it into a bag she carried across her body. Once they'd packed up, Caiden stood and pulled her chair out. Leaning this close to her he could smell her shampoo. Her shower soap too. She smelled like everything fresh and clean and good. His arms ached to pull her close and hold on.

When she stood, she turned and looked directly into his eyes. She ran her tongue along her lips to wet them and the lights from above reflected on the moisture. He had to struggle not to kiss her. The war he waged with himself was fierce and powerful. She was safe. Mia was alive.

He stepped away to allow her to pass, then he scooped up their breakfasts and walked behind her to the front door. Once outside he chanced a touch. Just a light touch at the small of her back. It was electric.

"My hotel is down on the strip."

She looked up at him. Indecision was written all over her face as she chewed on her bottom lip. He watched her waging a war with herself too, and he knew the feeling.

"I just want to talk to you."

She took a deep breath. "My apartment is three blocks away."

"Okay."

She continued walking and he stayed close. He was so afraid she'd take off running. So afraid he'd lose her again and never find her next time. But, he knew he'd have to be careful not to smother her. Not to scare her. He felt like he was lying on a bed of knives, afraid one wrong move would slice an artery.

They walked in silence for the first block, then the second block her phone rang, and she reached into her bag and pulled it out.

Holding up her phone, she said, "My boss."

He nodded and listened as she told her boss she wasn't feeling well and couldn't come in. She'd have her article to him as soon as she could, and then she compromised and said she'd come in tomorrow to catch up on what she missed. Once her call was over, she dropped her phone into her bag and continued walking.

"I was supposed to go into the office this morning for meetings."

"I'm glad you took the day off."

She nodded but said nothing. Her continued silence worried him and all the ugly rumors he'd heard about her over the years washed over him in a rush of feelings so strong he shook. Had she been the one who killed her mother? Had she been delirious on drugs? The questions flooded into his mind so strong he thought he'd lose his breath. He switched hands with the breakfasts he carried and pulled his inhaler from his right pocket and took a hit from it.

Mia turned and watched him, the concern in her eyes was comforting. "Are you alright?"

"I'm fine. I fried my lungs in an explosion in Afghanistan. I struggle to breathe sometimes."

She watched as he steadied his breathing, practiced inhaling and exhaling a couple of breaths. "I'm alright. We can continue."

She nodded and turned toward a tall, light brick building at the end of the street. "I live there." She pointed.

They entered the lobby and she pushed the button on the elevator while they waited in silence. The elevator opened and they silently stepped inside. His stomach knotted as the elevator rose. He knew he needed to be gentle, but he did want answers. He felt somewhat entitled to them. He was also worried he'd hate the answers. My God, what if he hated the answers?

4

Somewhere in the back of her mind she knew there would be a day when her past would meet her present. She'd tried to maintain as much anonymity as she could. In her profession, reporters were always vying for the spotlight; not Mia. She used an avatar for her picture in her articles, much to her boss' irritation. She'd claimed privacy, but she'd heard some of her coworkers talking about her. They joked that she was in witness protection and didn't want her picture taken. They were so close to the truth it wasn't funny.

She opened the door to her apartment and stepped inside. She wasn't afraid of Caiden. She'd never been afraid of him. She was afraid of his reaction to her explanation. She'd left without so much as a good-bye or a why.

Laying her laptop case on the small table to her right, she turned and watched Caiden's face as he entered her apartment. He was still tall and thin. Built, actually. He wore a long-sleeved t-shirt tucked into his jeans. His waist was trim but the muscles in his arms stretched the t-shirt material in beautiful ways. When they were in high school he worked out, but he wasn't as muscular as he was now.

He still carried their to-go boxes. "Should I put these in the refrigerator or do you want to eat now?"

"The fridge is fine."

She took their Styrofoam containers and as their fingers brushed she felt the current run up her arms. He was still exciting to touch. His blue eyes were crystal clear, his hair had darkened as he aged. He was a man built around the boy he'd been when she last saw him. But, she'd know him anywhere.

She took a deep breath. "Do you want coffee?"

"No."

"Okay. Please sit down. Let's make ourselves comfortable, because I have the feeling we'll be here a while."

He held his hand in front of him, waiting for her to proceed. Always the gentleman.

She swallowed as she passed him, suppressing the urge to inhale deeply. She could still smell his aftershave; it was no longer the boyish aftershave that smelled like something his grandfather would wear, but a scent that was both clean and enticing. She liked it.

Mia sat on one end of the sofa, Caiden sat at the opposite end. Her apartment was small and so was her sofa, but it allowed each of them the space they needed as they had this conversation.

"I'll just start by answering your questions from the diner." She swallowed. "I've been here for the most part since I left West Virginia. I had a few dollars to my name when I left. I hitchhiked to Wheeling." He gasped and she held up her hand. "I know. Stupid. But, I was scared. For my life. I had to get out of town and I had no way to do it but hitchhike."

"Mia. Why didn't you call me?"

"I didn't have the time Caiden. I literally ran."

"Why?"

"He killed my mom. I saw him do it. He said he'd kill me next. She fought. So hard." Tears spilled down her cheeks again. She swallowed and inhaled. "She fought so hard and with her dying breath she said, 'Run.' So, I did. I ran.

"I knew I only had a short amount of time and luck was with me. I flagged down a passing trucker as soon as I reached the edge of town and begged him to take me with him. He told me to hop in."

"Who killed your mom?"

"Dominick Nelson."

"Why? I don't understand any of this. Your mom was a good woman."

"Because of me. He killed her because of me." She swallowed. It felt like she'd begun to release a pressure valve.

"Mia. Why? Help me understand."

"After my dad took off, we needed money." She held up her hand when Caiden started to talk. "I know you asked me if we were alright, and I told you yes. I lied. I was embarrassed. Andrea told me she knew a way I could make some quick money and it wasn't gross. All I had to do was deliver a package for Dominick. She said he had a hard time finding people who could do it, and it was easy. So, I did. I made three hundred dollars delivering a small package for him. I didn't understand why he couldn't mail it. He just said the mail was too slow. So, I did it. Then I delivered another one a few days later. It was easy money. I couldn't believe it. Then Andrea came over about a week before my mom..." She swallowed and took a deep breath. Then she cleared her throat and began again.

"A week before my mom died, Andrea came over crying and told me we'd been stupid. The packages we were delivering were drugs. I didn't know we had drugs in Smoky Ridge. No one had talked about it and we were scared. Andrea said we'd go to jail if we got caught. Anyway, when Dominick called me to deliver another package for him, I told him I wouldn't do it. He yelled and bitched, then hung up on me. I thought that was it, I'd never hear from him again. But two days later, he showed up at my house just before I got home from school. When I walked in, he was standing behind my mother, holding on to her, with a knife at her throat. He told me I'd deliver packages for him or he'd kill her. I froze. I looked into my mom's eyes; tears ran down her cheeks. She was tired, she had bruises starting to form on her jaw, her cheeks, and her arms. He'd already beat her up. But my mom yelled, "No. Run!"

"I stood still. It was like I was frozen. I can still see the red line of blood where his knife sliced open her neck. Her eyes never left mine. She couldn't talk but she mouthed it again. 'Run.' So I did."

"Oh Mia." Caiden leaned forward and took her shaking hand. Her fingers curled into his as they sat in stony silence, while tears dripped down her cheeks. The vision of her mom's last moments on earth seared into her brain forever. The way her lips mouthed the word "Run." Saving Mia's life as her own drained away, lay like a stone in Mia's stomach every day since that day.

"So, you ran to the edge of town and found the truck driver?"

"Yes. I ran through backyards, and the woods for a ways, and around buildings, trying to stay as hidden as I could but get out of town. I didn't know if he had other people who would turn me in or find me. The trucker told me to get in and I did. I didn't tell him what happened, just that I needed to get far away. I drove with him to Las Vegas. At a gas station just outside of town he stopped to fuel up. I left fifty dollars on my seat for him, it was all I dared spare. I told him I had to go to the bathroom and I ducked out the back door. I asked at a restaurant for a YWCA—they let people rent a room there for very little money. I was able to find one, and my rent was only three dollars a night if I also mopped the floors. I did that for a couple of weeks until I found the job at a casino..."

"The Summit."

She looked into his eyes, surprised that he'd been tracking her down. "Yes." She cocked her head. "Royce?"

"Yes, but to be truthful, Royce wasn't ratting you out or anything. I asked questions. He wanted me to wait until he and Piper returned from their honeymoon and he said he'd put us in touch. I didn't want to wait. I couldn't wait."

His voice cracked, and her heart ached for what she'd put him through. What both of them had been through. She squeezed his fingers and when he squeezed hers in response, her heart raced faster.

"So, you got a job at The Summit?"

"Yes. It didn't pay a lot, but I was still at the Y and my rent was cheap. I waited tables and I ate most of my meals there. I took as many hours as they'd give me and by the time I'd been there just under a year, I'd saved a fair amount of money and I found a cheap apartment. Suzie, from The Summit, lived in the same building so I felt somewhat safe there. But, I always looked over my shoulder afraid that Nelson would find me. I met a kid at the Y that knew how to create a fake ID. I chose a new last name, and he made me legit. I used my social security number figuring no one would be able to search that. I finished high school by getting my GED. Then, I went to college partly on a scholarship and The Summit has an education program so that helped too."

"Why didn't you try to contact me, honey?"

"I was so afraid. And I figured you were better off without me. I would only bring trouble to you. You were going to go to college and be brilliant and own a business and I would have dragged you down."

When tears tracked down Caiden's cheeks, she came undone.

5

He scooted across the sofa and pulled Mia close. His heart hurt for her. For them. The reality of their lives, what they'd each been through, was what made them who they were today. True, in high school he'd dreamed of owning a construction business. He'd planned to go to school for structural design. Back home, their town was filled with houses nearing the century mark and he figured he'd come back with his education and begin to rehab those older homes.

But then Mia had left and he was filled with sorrow, anger, even rage some days. Especially the days in school where people were spreading all sorts of rumors about Mia being on drugs and killing her mom.

She lifted her head and softly asked, "I have no right to know, but what happened after I left?"

He inhaled as deeply as he could and swallowed to get his emotions in check.

"Andrea died about three weeks after you left. She overdosed. That's when the rumors intensified."

"Rumors...about me?"

"Yes. That you were the one who killed your mom while high on drugs."

Mia gasped. "How could anyone think that?"

She twisted on the sofa and looked at him. Her dark eyes glistened, framed by lashes spiked with moisture, and her nose was red from crying.

"People were scrambling. No one could find you and the police had been knocking on her door. They were convinced she was hiding you."

"Oh God. Her death is on my hands too."

Caiden shook his head, "No it isn't. That's on her. She confided in no one that I'm aware of as to the delivering of packages. I asked her countless times if she knew where you had gone or what had happened. I just couldn't get my head around it."

She took his hands in hers, her head bowed as they sat processing the information from the other. She sniffed a few times, then retrieved a box of tissues from a side table near a big picture window. Setting the box on the coffee table in front of them, she daintily blew her nose and carried the tissue to a wastebasket in the kitchen.

He heard the water turn on then off as she filled something with water. Caiden walked to the kitchen to watch her and found her making a pot of coffee.

"I could use some of this now. Not enough this morning."

He only nodded. He watched her throat as she put coffee in the pot, poured the water inside then set the pot on the burner and turned it on. She swallowed over and over again and he was doing the same thing.

"What about my brother? Where is he?"

Caiden leaned against the counter in the kitchen and stared at her refrigerator, devoid of pictures, mementos from vacations, or articles that families attached to their fridges.

Inhaling deeply, he said, "He's in a nursing home in Smoky Ridge."

She spun around, her eyes large her mouth open. "What? Why?"

Caiden shrugged, "He came home from college for your mom's funeral. He drove around and around looking for you. He called aunts and uncles asking about you. All your friends, everyone. One night he went out drinking, drove home, and had an accident. He suffered a head injury and he's confined to a wheelchair. I think your Aunt Rebecca is his guardian. Didn't you ever try looking anyone up on Google? Or the internet? You're a journalist."

Mia leaned against the counter on the opposite side of the kitchen from him. The small kitchen made their proximity close; her scent still wafted over to him. If he had to describe her condition at this point he'd say numb. At least, that's how he felt. It was a lot to process. All of it.

"No. I didn't want anyone ever to trace anything from Smoky Ridge to me here. I felt everyone was better off without me."

The freshly brewed coffee called to him and she still stood in a state of disbelief, staring at the stove across from her. Caiden opened cabinet doors until he found coffee cups and creamer and sugar, then he poured them each a cup, added creamer to his, but nothing to hers. At the diner she'd had black coffee, though he wasn't sure about sugar. He handed her a cup and she slowly took it from his hand but didn't sip it. He sipped at his, closed his eyes and paid attention to how the coffee felt sliding down his throat. It was better than swallowing the bitter pills he'd been swallowing for most of his life.

Finally, she lifted her cup to her lips and sipped, then she inhaled and looked up at him. "What about you, Caiden. What have you done with your life? Did you go to college? Get married?"

He stared at her a moment, watching for a sign that she was mocking him or mad that his life had gone on without her. He didn't get that feeling from her, though he did feel like she was bracing herself for the answers in case she hated them. "No to college. After you disappeared, and Andrea died, then your brother's accident, life was crashing in on me. An Army recruiter came to school to speak to us about the military, and I signed up on the spur of the moment. At that time it felt like I needed to be run ragged and not have to think. Letting some drill sergeant yell at me all day seemed safer and easier than making decisions on my own at that time. I left for the Army two days after graduation."

"And you were in an explosion?"

She swallowed as she waited.

"Yeah, I had served eight years... Then I re-upped again... I actually enjoyed a lot about the Army and was proud to serve my country. During my last deployment, we were on a recon mission and the vehicle in front of mine hit an IED. We were engulfed in flames. My lungs were singed as a result of the fire, but we were lucky to get out. I was sent home to recuperate."

She sipped her coffee but watched his face, his eyes, and he couldn't look away from hers. "And now you rescue women who are being trafficked."

He shrugged. "Something like that. We hunt down pedophiles too. Because of my breathing issues, it's difficult to be in the field, so I'm usually on the computer. But this particular mission is taking all of us on the team to wrap up and I was called in." He watched her face as he explained his job, then commented, "And you also try to help women and children."

She bit her bottom lip, "I do what I can. I was taken advantage of by Dominick, my mother was murdered, my father took off and left us. I feel like helping them is a way to give back. I've always wanted to write, and this way I'm bringing awareness to how prevalent trafficking is. I don't think a lot of people know it's such a huge business."

He nodded. "That's a fact."

He inhaled once again; his chest felt like a weight was lying on it, but that was likely just all the emotions he was feeling.

Then he asked, "Where do we go from here?"

6

Mia took a deep breath. "You didn't answer me earlier. Are you married? Did you ever marry?"

"No."

"Just no. You never found anyone..."

"No."

She fidgeted with a seam in her slacks. "I'm sorry."

"I am too."

When she looked into his eyes his expression was unreadable. "Do you know if Dominick Nelson is still alive and running his operation?"

Caiden rinsed his cup in the sink, then set it down. "I honestly don't know. I didn't know he existed until today. His drug operation was so far from my radar I'm stunned to hear about it. I also didn't know to seek him out." He turned to her. "Why did you only change your last name?"

"That's an abrupt change of subject." She set her cup in the sink next to his then walked past him and out to the living room again. "It was another way of hiding in plain sight. Like he'd expect me to change my name, so I only changed my last name."

His eyebrows rose and he grinned. "That actually makes sense."

She chuckled, "Thanks. I'm not a good fugitive, but I figured by coming here it was easier to blend in and escape into the throngs of people if I saw someone who scared me."

"You're a pretty good fugitive, I'd say. You've managed to stay hidden for, what is it now, sixteen years or so?"

His tone had a bit of an edge to it and she froze. After a beat she continued on to the sofa and took her seat on the end. "Yes. About sixteen years."

"Did you ever plan on showing up at home again?"

"No."

"So, you're happy everyone thinks you're a fugitive murderer?"

She looked into his eyes. What did she expect? Of course, there'd be an edge to his tone—the shock had worn off.

"I'm certainly not happy I'm considered a murderer. Absolutely not. But, if I go back, Dominick will find me and kill me just like he killed my mom."

Caiden shrugged, walked back to the sofa and sat down again. He turned to face her and took a deep breath. "Do you want to go back?"

She shook her head slowly but said nothing.

"If you knew it was safe, would you want to go back?"

She swallowed a lump in her dry throat; all those emotions that had been swirling and building as bad news upon bad news had bombarded her brain had landed in her throat, threatening to suffocate her.

"I'd want to see my brother." Caiden nodded and let out a breath. "And I'd want to visit my mom's grave."

His eyes bore into hers and his jaw twitched.

"Do you go back?"

"I didn't for the first few years. I saved money and flew my parents out to me when I had leave. Or I'd meet them somewhere else, like Myrtle Beach or Disney or somewhere. But, my dad got sick about five years ago and I went back to be with him and help my mom."

"Is he alright?"

"He got better, but he's never recovered all his strength. He has a bad heart. They don't travel anymore. So I try to get home twice a year and I call them every week."

She couldn't stop looking into his eyes. The same deep blue she remembered, and looking into them now, she could almost imagine they were back in high school, sitting at a basketball game in the gym, their favorite spot at the very top, in the upper right corner of the bleachers, cheering on their team. Caiden didn't play basketball; he was built for football and track.

"That's wonderful." She tucked her hair behind her ear and thought about finding a hair-tie to pull it back. She felt like she was wearing lead shoes and every move would require so much more energy than she had right now.

"Tell me about your writing." His lips formed a half smile.

"After I graduated from college, Barry, a co-worker from The Summit..."

"Does he tend bar?"

She took in a breath as she stared at him. "I shouldn't be surprised, I guess, that you've done some research on me."

"I wouldn't call it research. I didn't want to wait until Royce and Piper returned so I badgered him to tell me how I could find you."

She chuckled, "How did you badger him?"

"I called him three times a day while he's on his honeymoon. He told me he didn't know much about you other than you worked at the paper, and he had your phone number, which he wouldn't give out. I think he figured he'd keep me busy by telling me you used to work at The Summit. So, I went there."

Mia rotated her head on her shoulders to ease some of the stiffness that had been present since Caiden showed up at the diner. "Anyway, Barry knew the editor of the newspaper and set up an interview for me."

Caiden leaned back into the arm of the sofa. He was trying to look casual, but his tension was evident. The muscled cords on his arms were tight and she saw him flex his fingers here and there to relieve some tension. When he said nothing, she continued.

"I took some of my articles into my interview and he was impressed. I got a job, at first only part-time and very limited. He sent me out and about to report on new restaurants opening—there is always a new business of some sort opening here in Vegas. But I had to go out and get the scoop. I did that for a couple of months and as luck would have it, a full-time reporter with the paper quit in a huff one day. My editor called me in and offered me the job. I took it. I reported on bigger events happening in Vegas, but also added human interest to the stories. Something about the owner or the 'why' behind the business type stuff. That's how I met my first subject for my first trafficking story. She opened a gift shop on the strip. She was a survivor and I was captivated by her story. I also realized how incredibly lucky I'd been in not being forced into that life. While my story is awful, it isn't nearly as horrible as it could have been. Through her, I've met dozens of women who have gone through similar things. I write their stories to get the word out."

7

"I could help you Mia." Her eyes flicked to his, her forehead wrinkled. "I can help you find out if Nelson is still alive. If he's still running his operation. And, if he is, I can work with my team to get him shut down. And brought to justice for killing your mom."

She stared at him but said nothing. She didn't move a muscle, she was a gorgeous frozen statue whose eyes held such fear and dread and heartbreak. Then the tears appeared, first in her left eye, then in her right and he watched them as they spilled over the corner of her eyes and made wet tracks on her smooth cheeks.

It was long moments and the tears seemed as though they'd never end before her lips trembled. Her tongue swiped along her lips to wet them and he watched as she swallowed. Finally she leaned forward and pulled a tissue from the box she'd placed on the coffee table earlier. They were so still, and the room was so quiet, the swish from the tissue being pulled from the cardboard seemed like it was on high volume.

Mia dried her tears and daintily blew her nose. As she rose to toss the tissue in the kitchen, he noticed for the first time that her entrance door had three locks on it. He stared at those, one deadbolt, and two slide locks. There was a reinforced steel wrap around the door handle and lock to help prevent someone prying a door open or prying a lock loose.

He stood and walked to the windows across from the door that looked outside over the street below. They were on the third floor of her apartment building, which was six stories high. The outdoor balconies from the apartments on either side of Mia's had colored chairs and plants on them, but Mia didn't have a balcony.

"What are you looking at?"

Glancing over his shoulder at Mia he looked back outside at the edges of the balconies. "You don't have a balcony."

"No."

"I guess I didn't notice when we walked here that some of the apartments didn't have them."

"Some don't. I specifically chose this apartment because it didn't have one. I had the choice of three when I moved here."

Caiden turned to face her, his hands tucked into the front pockets of his jeans. "Why did you pick an apartment without a balcony?"

"I didn't want to make it easy for Dominick to send someone up here and break in."

"Is that why you have all the locks on the doors?"

"Yes." She glanced quickly at her door then back to him. "I had them installed, all except the one slide lock that was on the door when I moved in. I had the security panel placed over the lock and behind the doorknob. I added the deadbolt and the additional slide lock. For the first few years, I had a narrow plant stand on the wall next to the door that I kept a jar filled with marbles and bells. I'd slide that over in front of the door each night before I went to bed. If someone did manage to get past all the locks, they'd knock over the table with the jar of marbles on it and make noise. It would give me enough time to protect myself."

"How would you protect yourself Mia?"

She swallowed and her fingers fidgeted at the seam of her slacks. "I got my concealed-carry permit, I joined a women's shooting club, I practice every week. I own a few guns, I carry, and have them hidden inside for my protection."

His eyes roamed down her body, then back up to her eyes. She watched his eyes and seemed a bit uneasy at his perusal but made no move to show him where she was carrying.

"Are you carrying now?"

She swallowed then lightly sniffed. "Yes."

He smiled at her. "You carry well. I can't see it and you aren't imprinting at all. Nice job."

When her eyes roamed his body his cock thickened. He remembered the first time they had sex and he remembered how she felt. It was the first time for both of them and it was a moment in time he'd never ever forget. He watched to see if she noticed his cock moving in his jeans, but she made no expression to say she did or she didn't.

"Are you carrying?" Her voice was soft when she asked.

"Yes. In my line of work, I never go anywhere without a gun or two."

She nodded. Then she smiled and he couldn't stop staring at her transformation. The happy light flickered to life in her eyes. "You carry well, and you aren't imprinting."

He laughed and then so did she. It felt good.

"So, let's get back to my question and my statement. Where do we go from here? Let me help you clear your name and see your brother once again."

"How?"

"Mia, we have resources. Let me help you."

It took her a long time to answer but when she did, it was as if a huge weight was lifted from his shoulders. "Okay."

He smiled and she smiled in return. He wanted to run across the room and scoop her into his arms and hold on forever. His arms ached to hold her. His heart—fuck, his heart for the first time in years—felt a bit of peace.

"Now, where do we go?" He asked.

"Where do you want to go Caiden?"

He moved away from the window a few steps, just enough to see her clearer. He wanted to smell her scent again. He wanted to touch her. "I'm not going to lie. My feelings are a jumble of things right now. Anger. Frustration. Relief.

Hurt. Hope. So many. And my mind is struggling to process all of it. But, if you can give me a day or two to do some digging on Nelson and see what I can find out, I'd say that's a good place to start. After that, let's see how we are both feeling."

"That's fair." She shook her head. "It's more than I could ever ask for."

8

Mia cleaned up the kitchen, poured the leftover coffee down the drain, rinsed the pot and made the next pot for tomorrow, setting the timer to go off at five. Caiden was using the bathroom and she was grateful for a few moments to gather her thoughts.

Caiden was going to look into Dominick. And, maybe, just maybe, she'd be able to go back home and visit her brother. Let him know she was still alive. But, after all the time and what he'd suffered, would he want to see her? He might be so mad that she'd do him more harm than good.

The toilet flushed, the faucet turned on...then off after he washed his hands and she turned to face the hall as he walked out. He walked past the kitchen, then stopped and turned to see her standing there waiting for him.

"So, I've been thinking. Right now, we're looking for someone here in town that we know is involved in the trafficking of the women you interviewed as well as many others. That's why I'm still here in town and my team member Creed Rowan is still here too. But, I'll have some time to gather intel on Nelson. And Creed will help, I'm sure of it. When we're in the field, we often have large blocks of time while we're waiting on reports or intel from headquarters. And, since we're both a bit stir-crazy sitting in a hotel room, we'll spend it working up a file on Nelson."

"What does that cost? I mean, I can pay for..."

"No. Let's not make it a financial thing."

She stared at his face, so many emotions ran across his handsome features and she felt like she could name them all. He was holding back, but not. He was wrestling with his emotions. But so was she.

"Okay." She tucked her hair behind her ear. "Thank you."

"I'm going to need you to come to the hotel with me, so Creed and I can ask you questions about Dominick and the day your mom died. The more we have the more we can dig."

She swallowed and her throat felt like she'd swallowed sand. A pit grew hot in the bottom of her stomach and her breathing came in shallow huffs. When she answered him, it was barely discernible. "Okay."

"Can you go now?"

Mia turned and looked at the clock on her stove. It was now ten-thirty. They'd been here talking for almost three hours. "Yes."

Caiden nodded, stared for a moment, then turned and walked to the living room. He stood waiting for her to gather her things, but what she most needed to gather were her courage and her wits. How did one gather those?

She took a deep breath and walked into the living room. She picked up her purse and slung it over her head, the long cross-body strap allowing her bag to hang unattended. Then she picked up her computer bag and hung that on her right shoulder. She turned to Caiden, who stood watching her, and her heartbeat sped up. Suddenly she couldn't tell what his emotions were. His jaw tightened and released, and she felt like he was holding something back. He hadn't yelled at her for being gone. He hadn't bothered to rail and bitch as she assumed anyone would. That too, was a puzzle.

She walked to the door and opened the locks. Caiden came up behind her and she could smell his aftershave again. Oh, she liked how he smelled.

Stepping into the hallway she waited until Caiden exited, then she turned and locked the deadbolt and the lock on the doorknob.

Caiden walked ahead and pushed the button for the elevator and stood silently waiting for her. As they stepped inside she felt conspicuous, as if anyone within eyesight of her would know she carried a huge secret. She remembered that feeling when she first left home. As if everyone would look at her and know she wasn't who she said she was. Working as a waitress she'd had that feeling often, but as time went on and no one recognized her, she grew more and more confident that her plan had succeeded, and she let her guard down. A bit. Not completely. Never, completely.

The doors opened once again at the lobby and they stepped off the elevator. Her phone buzzed in her purse and she pulled it from the outer pocket and froze.

She read the words on the screen, then her vision floated as tears formed in her eyes.

She didn't hear Caiden ask her a question, she stared at the offensive words on her phone, frozen in time as if she'd seen Medusa.

"Mia? What's wrong?"

Blinking she turned her phone to Caiden and showed him the text. She'd never gotten a threatening text before. How did one handle that?

"Who's it from?"

She couldn't form a word, so he gently took her phone from her hand and searched the text. She let him play around with it, whatever he was doing.

"Okay. I've forwarded it to me and to Creed. Let's get going."

"After all these years, why am I receiving threats now?"

"Because you dared to interview women and get their story out. You're giving them a voice and someone doesn't like it very much."

He took her hand and she loved the warmth of his larger hand holding her smaller one. His hand was gentle but strong, rough where hers was soft.

"Let's go honey."

Tilting her head up to see his face this close; her eyes met his and held. His lashes were still the long dark lashes that framed those gorgeous blue eyes. There were lines at the corners now where none had been when she knew him before. But they added character and interest and likely were due to worry over the years. His father, mother and probably her too.

Mia stepped forward to go with him and was happy he continued to hold her hand. Her knees shook and maybe taking a good walk would help regain her composure.

9

He slowed his stride so Mia didn't have to run to keep up, then he noticed that she jostled her computer bag and he felt foolish.

"Let me carry that for you."

"No. It's okay."

"It's not, honey." He stopped and held his hand out to take her laptop case. She hesitated and bit her bottom lip but finally relented and pulled it from her shoulder and handed it to him. "How do you normally get around town?"

"I have a car."

"Where is it?"

"In the garage in the basement of the complex."

"Can you drive us back to the hotel? It's close to a five-mile walk."

"Yes."

She turned and walked back toward her apartment building and Caiden stayed close. She had gotten a death threat and while it could very likely be only a threat from someone pissed off about her article, they'd managed to get her phone number.

"Do you get calls on your articles often?"

"Sometimes. Usually from women who have been in the same or a similar situation and want their story told too."

They crossed the street and Caiden looked around to make sure there wasn't anyone watching them. That's when he saw him. Dildo. Sergeant Dilano. The man they've been looking for. And he was standing by the corner of Mia's apartment complex, as if he was waiting for her.

Caiden stopped and stared at him and Dilano nodded his skeevy head, then turned and walked away. Caiden had to make a split-second decision to run after him, which he couldn't do for very long, and which would also leave Mia alone, or do nothing. In the end he pulled his phone from his pocket and snapped a few pictures of Dilano and forwarded them to Emmy. "He's still here."

He got a thumbs-up in return. He then pulled up the pictures he'd just taken and showed them to Mia.

"Have you ever seen this man?"

She looked at the pictures, her fingers spreading the photo larger to see his face clearer, then she shook her head. "No, I've never seen him."

"Well, if you do, stay away. Far away. He's one of the men we're looking for who is involved in the trafficking. And it's suspicious that he's here, by your building around the same time you get a threatening text. It doesn't take a genius to figure he might be onto who you are, and you may be his target now."

Mia's eyes rounded and the utter fear on her face made him feel bad for her. But she needed to hear this and after the life she'd led, it wasn't something new. Just a new nemesis.

"Shit."

"Right. Let's get to your car."

They walked across the street, Caiden ever vigilant about their surroundings and the people they were in close proximity to. No one else seemed interested in them, but that didn't always mean anything. He held Mia's hand tightly, as if that made any difference if someone wanted to shoot at them, but he held on just the same. They rounded the side of the building and she led them to a doorway that led to a staircase which descended down into the parking garage.

The dark garage made him uneasy but three steps in and the lights flickered on.

"Is there more than one floor?"

"No. Just this one. I'm over here."

She led him to the left and the far row along the wall. The garage held four rows of cars, lined up at an angle, the arrows in bright yellow painted on the floor directing drivers to the exit.

She stopped and pulled keys from her purse, then pressed a button on the fob, the lights flashed, and a chirp emitted from a Jeep Wrangler. It was older, but in pristine shape. Only two doors which allowed it to fit well in the garage. Mia stopped then and handed him the keys. "Do you mind driving? My hands are shaking and..."

"Not at all."

He took the keys from her hand and forced himself to ignore the electric current that ran up his arm when their fingers brushed. He wondered if she felt it too because her lips quivered, and he heard a slight intake of breath. He shook his head, that would need to be processed later, right now they needed to get to the hotel, where first of all he had some backup and where Dilano didn't know where they were. He clearly now knew where Mia lived.

He opened the passenger door and waited for Mia to step inside. He tucked her laptop behind her seat then closed the door and walked around the rear end and to the driver's door, his eyes scanning the garage for foes.

As soon as he closed the driver's door, he started her Jeep up and backed out of her space, noting that her apartment number was painted on the wall in front of the Jeep. Not exactly safe.

Caiden pulled from the garage, and headed toward their hotel, ever vigilant for Dildo lurking nearby. How he had found Mia so easily was a bit scary as to what kind of power he had and the resources at his disposal.

As soon as he pulled in at the hotel, a valet came to give him a ticket, which he pocketed, and walked around to help Mia out. He reached in and pulled out her laptop, then took her hand and hustled them inside. They hurried to an elevator and his heart raced the closer they got to what he felt was safety.

They exited on the fifth floor, hustled down the hall quietly as they neared his room, and he pulled the room card from his back pocket.

He opened the door and stepped back to allow Mia to enter first then quickly stepped in and closed the door. Creed sat at the desk on the computer and nodded in his direction.

"Creed this is Mia. Mia, Creed is one of my co-workers."

"Hi Creed. It's nice to meet you."

"Nice to meet you too Mia." Creed then looked up at him. "So Emmy texted and I got your pictures and I've been trying to track him with cameras from area businesses. He headed down the street away from downtown on foot. I lost him at just past the convenience store five blocks away."

"Shit. Okay. Well, we know he's still here and we know what kind of car he drove based on the information the American women gave us from the container."

"Right. I'm searching area car rental places to see if he rented that car. Not sure if it's his private car or a rental but I figure we can rule it out."

Creed looked over at Mia. "I'm sorry to say you won't be able to go back to your apartment tonight. He knows where you live now."

"But, I didn't bring anything to change into."

"I'm sorry, but it can't be helped."

Creed looked up at him. "Did we keep Piper's room when Diego and Falcon left?"

"I'll check."

Caiden pulled his phone from his pocket and dialed the front desk asking about the availability of the room next to theirs.

"Piper's old room is still available."

Into his phone he said, "Yes, we'll take it. Thank you."

He smiled at Mia. "I'll feel better knowing you're right next door. The rooms are adjoining so we'll be able to keep you safe."

10

Mia sat at the foot of the bed in Caiden and Creed's room as she waited for someone to come up and bring her a key to the room next door. She felt like she'd felt all those years ago when she'd run from Smoky Ridge. Lost. Afraid. Alone. Her mouth felt like she'd stuffed it with cotton and her tongue stuck to the roof of her mouth. Her heartbeat had finally slowed, and she barely listened as Caiden and Creed chatted about locations and cameras and possible partners and coordinates. Caiden received a couple of calls on his phone and she stared straight ahead as her mind whirled. She'd honestly thought this part of her life was over. But in a cruel twist of fate, she was right back at the beginning, when she'd run from a murderer who was searching for her. How many times did that happen in a regular person's life? She could count two.

"Mia?"

She looked up at Caiden, who stood in front of her, worry imprinted on his handsome face.

"I'm sorry. What?"

"Room service is here with your key, are you ready?"

"Oh. Sure."

She stood and her knees felt as though they would buckle. "You okay?"

"Um. Yeah." She swallowed. "Yes."

Caiden took her hand and led her out the door. They walked to the next room over and he waved the key card in front of the panel on the door. Her heartbeat sped up as he opened the door then stepped back so she could enter first. The room was a mirror image of the one Caiden and Creed were in. Same bedding, curtains, and furniture. It was oddly comforting.

Caiden walked to the door that connected the two rooms and opened it. "Please leave this door open so I can be sure you're alright. We won't bother you if you don't want to speak with us. But I need to make sure you're safe. Can you do that?"

She nodded. "Yes."

He set her laptop bag on the desk and turned to face her. "I can give you a couple of t-shirts to sleep in. And you can wash your things in the sink in the bathroom. We'll take care of lunch and dinner for tonight. As we gather more information, we'll update you."

"Okay."

She walked to the window and looked down on the strip. People walked back and forth without worry and she wondered if this Dilano-what did Caiden call him-Dildo was watching her right now. Or at a minimum, looking for her.

A shiver ran down her spine. She turned to see Caiden was gone. Panic rose up in her throat and her stomach roiled. Mia paced to the adjoining door; Caiden sat on the foot of the bed she'd just vacated with a laptop, typing away as Creed read off some coordinates. He glanced up at her and stopped typing.

"You're welcome to join us Mia, I just didn't want to intrude on your privacy." He nodded to the door. "Such as it is."

"Thank you. Who is this Dilano person?" She stepped into the room but leaned against the wall.

Caiden and Creed shared a glance before Caiden answered. "He's someone we used to work for. Until we found out he was crooked. We've been searching for him for about a year and a half. We honestly didn't know just how deep he was in with the trafficking, but we should have suspected. His ability to evade capture means he has help and means and money.

"And you're sure he is involved in the trafficking of the women I interviewed from Container World?"

"Yes. We're sure. We saw him there, though he had a vehicle stashed and was able to run before we could turn our attention to him."

"But he stuck around town. Why?"

Creed stopped typing and looked her in the eye. "We're not completely sure other than he sought to hide in plain sight and his work here isn't finished. And, it's plausible that he recognized us, and read your interviews, and saw your mention of RAPTOR, and has an axe to grind."

"With you or with me?"

Caiden set his laptop to the side and looked up at her. "Could be both. We don't know until we capture him."

"Okay." She took a deep breath, then sat on the bench next to her. "What can I do to help?"

Caiden stared for a few beats, then smiled. "Okay, let's start with whether any of the women referred to Dilano at all. Either by calling him Sergeant, Dilano, or both. Did any of the women mention anyone other than Easton, Haywood, and Dawson?"

Mia thought for a moment. "Let me grab my laptop and check my notes. I may have something written down that didn't seem important at the time."

Caiden smiled and nodded, picked his laptop up and began working again.

She pulled her computer from its case and the notebook she also carried for other notes when her computer wasn't convenient. She inhaled a few deep breaths and exhaled. Nerves settled again, she rejoined the men. She'd do what she could to help them and not continue to be a victim. Then, hopefully Caiden was serious, and he'd help her find out if Dominick was still in business or still in Smoky Ridge, and she'd stop being his victim and actively work to bring him down too. Finally, after all these years, she felt like she was on the brink of being the person she always wanted to be. A smile formed on her lips and her heart raced at the possibilities.

"What are you smiling for?" Caiden asked.

When she looked up she saw him staring at her and the look in his eyes was...wow.

"I finally feel like a whole person. Like I'll be a whole person. I've never had this feeling before. I've always been weighed down with the need for invisibility. Doing only what I thought I could do without being found out. But, something just came over me. I'm a caterpillar about to become a butterfly."

11

Caiden smiled as he watched Mia. She read her notes and then glanced at her notebook, but mostly she looked completely engrossed in her work and there was a peacefulness that had settled over her. But in a weird energetic way.

His phone buzzed and he picked it up off the bed and read a text from Emmy. "If you see Dildo again, follow him. He's so close, we can't let him get away again."

He responded quickly. "Roger."

Then looked at Creed. "Creed, Emmy says if we see Dildo again, we're to follow him. She doesn't want him getting away again."

"Roger." Creed kept typing and clicking with his mouse.

Caiden continued his work, which was hacking into the security system and camera feed at Container World. They'd declined to share their video, instead telling police they'd need a court order. The police were working on it but that all took so much time. In the meantime, they didn't have the time to wait for the legal system to do its job, so Caiden decided to push things along a bit. He was sooo close...

"Got it." He yelled. Creed came to stand over his shoulder. "I did it. I've gotten into Container World's system."

He clicked around and found the video feed storage, then called up the night they'd rescued the women, which was seven days ago. Most of these systems only kept video for two weeks, some of them a month, so time was a factor here.

He found the date. "Here it is."

Mia came to sit next to him and look over his other shoulder. He played the video of the night they'd gone in, speeding it up, times two, to get to the times they saw any movement.

Creed leaned in to see the grainy video, "Stop it there!"

Caiden froze the video, then backed it up a few seconds then played at normal speed.

"Who's that?" Mia asked.

"That's Haywood."

"Is he carrying Piper there?" Mia asked as she watched the screen.

"Yes. She was dressed for a gala that she and Royce went to."

Mia nodded and he could feel her breath on his jaw when she responded. "That's right. I remember that now."

Creed turned to stare at her and she shrugged. "I focused mostly on the women who were rescued, and Piper declined an interview because she wanted to remain anonymous."

Creed nodded and Caiden remembered Piper saying she wanted the focus to be on the women, not her; she was doing her job.

They watched as Haywood carried Piper into the container, then stepped out alone and locked it up. Time passed, close to an hour on the video, when off to the left of the screen a dark vehicle pulled up just outside of the fence and stopped. Caiden froze the video then turned to Creed.

"You focus on the vehicle, I'm going to focus on the containers."

Mia, not to be left out, added, "I'll focus on the women."

Caiden smiled and nodded, then started the video once again.

"There he is." Creed said, pointing to the man walking toward the containers.

Caiden slowed the video down and they watched as Dildo walked right into the yard at Container World and walked directly to the container that held Piper. Haywood opened the container and Dildo walked inside for a few minutes, then stepped out holding Piper by the arm, a hood over her head, and pulled her to the next container. She'd looked groggy and her posture was stiff, which meant she'd likely bent wrong and felt the sharpness of the shrapnel touching a nerve, they'd heard her cry out on the microphone hidden in her necklace. Caiden clenched his jaw as he watched the rough treatment she'd endured. Piper had never let on about how roughly she'd been handled.

Creed muttered. "Fuck."

Caiden only nodded as they both watched Piper being pulled inside the other container.

Haywood locked the container and the two men stood outside talking.

"This is where she told us on her mic that she was moved." Creed added.

Haywood then turned and Dawson walked to them. He looked at his watch, shrugged and they all looked around, then walked toward the front of Container World.

"They must have been waiting for a transport vehicle."

Caiden slowed the video again, "There we are."

Creed cut the lock with a bolt cutter, opened the doors, then he and Falcon Montgomery, another teammate, stood with their backs to the doors as Royce entered the container. Creed looked in and then stepped in a few seconds later with his bolt cutter.

Mia exclaimed, "There they are. The first one is Piper, then Marie. That one is Sherry and there's Eleese."

She put her hand over her stomach. They watched as Piper went to the container she'd first come out of and pounded on it. There was no sound so they couldn't hear what was happening, but just watching it was giving him angst.

The women began to emerge, their team began bringing them to safety, then you could see the tiny flame shoot from the ends of their guns as the fighting broke out. His heart hammered in his chest as he watched Haywood run up from behind and Dawson move toward them.

“Oh my God.” Mia said softly, her hand still over her belly.

Soon Haywood was lying dead between the containers; Dawson had been shot but was still alive, and Caiden strained his eyes to see where Dildo went.

“There he goes, that fucker.” He pointed at the screen.

Dildo jumped the fence and took off in the vehicle he had hidden alongside, and he and Piper struggled to keep up, which made him feel like a failure. Watching how close they were, he swallowed the sour taste in his mouth and his head hung down. Mia’s hand slid over to his on the bed and squeezed, his face burned bright with embarrassment.

Creed chucked him from the back. “Don’t do that. It’s the reason we’re all with RAPTOR. All of us have something.”

Mia looked over at Creed, her brows pulled together, and Creed stepped from between the beds and pulled up the right pant leg of his jeans to show her his prosthetic.

“Wow. You don’t even limp.”

Creed shrugged. “Thanks.”

“So, you’re all wounded veterans?”

Caiden looked into her eyes as he explained. “Yes. All of us were drafted into a program called Operation Live Again and retrained based on our abilities. Because I struggle to breathe when running, they put me behind the computer."

"Plus he's good at it. They all are; Caiden, Piper, and Deacon."

Caiden looked over at his teammate and nodded. "We're all good at our jobs. There's none better."

"Now, we just have to prove it and find Dildo."

12

Mia read through her notes and her heart raced just like it did when she'd written everything down. While their stories had been so similar to so many others' stories, she was interviewing them immediately after they'd been rescued. They still had the stench of the container and their deplorable conditions on them. Their emotions were so raw and fresh it made her fingers shake. Their gratitude for being rescued was repeated over and over, as well as their fear that they'd have to go back. The utter urgency in their voices as they asked the bus driver to go—get them out of there before their captors came back- was frightening and gut-wrenching.

She also had her recorder, which she'd left at the office and she'd need to retrieve. The interviews had already been transcribed, most of them were anyway, but since she'd been focused on getting the story out and not on the fine details of it, she could very well have overlooked something that might be important to Caiden and Creed.

Reading the stories of the women brought it all back to her once again, she'd been so fortunate she hadn't fallen into trafficking like these poor women had. She flipped through her notebook, focusing on the American women, because the Russian women had been locked in a container since they'd arrived in the US.

She looked up at Caiden, "Just a thought, but do you have access to records as to whether Dildo has ever left the country?"

"We've checked, but unless he's flying privately or under an alias, we couldn't find anything on him. Why?"

"I just wondered if someone flew over to Russia to approve the women they're bringing here or if it's on the trust system. For instance, if the purpose to bring them here is to keep them disoriented and in unfamiliar surroundings so they don't run, what if they bring over prostitutes and vagrants that aren't of a quality to sell just to get the body count they need? In the meantime, the exchange of prime women from here, and that's an assumption on our part, is already on the way to Russia. And, what is their guarantee that the women coming from here are prime women, so to speak?" She swallowed the lump in her throat. "Women who would earn them good money."

Caiden nodded, "I can run a search for repeated flights to and from the US to Russia and vice-versa. Last time I did that, I found too many to go through. There are thousands of businessmen and women who go back and forth for work. Without specific parameters, the list would have to be gone over line by line."

Mia looked up, "Wait!"

She flipped back through her notes. "Women. You're going to think this is off the wall, but one of the women, Vika, said something about Nadia. I thought she meant one of the other women you'd rescued. Now that I'm looking at my notes, I didn't interview anyone named Nadia."

Caiden began typing furiously into his computer. She watched his eyes scan the screen and his finger scroll with his mouse.

"I think you're on to something Mia. Let me run a search on the reports I downloaded on the flights to and from Russia to see if a Nadia is on them."

Mia's fingers began to shake. She hoped she was correct and she wasn't leading them on a wild-goose chase; every moment counted.

Caiden began clicking with his mouse furiously. "You're definitely on to something Mia." Creed walked over to peer over Caiden's shoulder and Mia did the same. "Right here." Caiden pointed.

On Caiden's computer screen were yellow highlighted sections with the name Nadia Petrov.

Creed went back to his computer and started tapping away. Mia continued to look over Caiden's shoulder. Partly to see what he was doing and partly, maybe mostly, because she could inhale his scent. Her feelings for him hadn't vanished. And watching him now, so engrossed in his work...his shoulder muscles rippled and moved as he worked. He'd bulked up since she'd known him last, his chest was broad, his shoulders filled with muscles and sinew.

He turned his head to look at her and she was so close to his lips, she could just lean in and touch his lips to hers. Just a quick kiss. Only to connect on that level to him. What would he do? Did he want her to make the effort first?

Creed broke the spell. "I have Van working up a file on Nadia Petrov."

Caiden turned his head to look at Creed. "Thanks Creed. I hope that helps us get a bit closer to ending this ring."

Caiden continued highlighting Nadia Petrov's name on the list he had in front of him and Mia reluctantly pulled herself away. She went back to her notes and her computer and began searching for Nadia Petrov's name herself, to see if there were any other mentions of her that may be of assistance. To say she was excited was an understatement. This feeling, it was a feeling she'd never had before. She was making a difference.

She slightly shook her head to get it in the game, then inhaled and let it out slowly as she focused once again on her notes, intending to first read through her handwritten notes, then her typed notes. Maybe later on today Caiden would walk with her to her office and she'd retrieve her recorder.

Her phone buzzed and she glanced at the screen. "You can't hide forever." The number said, "Unknown."

Her heartbeat increased and her fingers shook, as she picked it up and opened the text to see if there was anything else in it.

"Is it another threatening text?"

She looked up to see Caiden's worried face staring at her.

Mia swallowed a lump then nodded slowly. She didn't need to say anything more. Caiden stood and walked to her, picked up her phone and read the text. He turned the phone to Creed, who tightened his jaw and inhaled deeply.

"Fucker."

13

Caiden tapped out a response to this coward: "What do you want? I'll meet with you to give you what you want."

To harass a woman and scare her for pleasure was a bullshit thing to do. To harass and scare Mia, well, that didn't sit well.

The three dots bounced as a reply was typed out. He glanced over to Mia, who sat staring at him. She swallowed and her chest rose with the intake of breath. Her phone buzzed in his hand and he looked down to read the reply.

"I'll meet you. Alone. I want all your notes on the Container World article."

Caiden quickly responded. "Okay."

He stared at Mia's phone; the dots weren't bouncing. "Creed, I'm setting up a meeting."

"Perfect."

When a text didn't appear right away, he resumed his seat on the foot of the bed and picked up his laptop once again. He set Mia's phone next to him so he could respond to a text the moment it came in.

"Caiden?"

His eyes landed on Mia.

"I can protect myself. I know what Dilano looks like and I'll stay away from him. But I need to work. I need to pack a couple of things from home. And I need to run to the newspaper and pick up my recorder."

"I can't let you leave here without Creed or myself. For a couple of reasons. One, we're now on a mission. We know Dilano is here, that means we're actively searching for him. I can't risk that you'll cause us to lose him..."

Mia opened her mouth to say something, but Caiden held his hand up. "Let me finish please."

Mia crossed her arms in front of her.

"Mia, honey, it's so much more dangerous than you imagine. I know you've been through a lot. I know you've been able to keep yourself safe. But, when we're close to an investigation like this, it gets so much more dangerous than you can imagine. Fear of being arrested takes over and these perps don't care who gets in the way, they will do anything to avoid getting caught. Anything."

Creed turned in his chair. "Mia, Caid's right. Let us play this out. Let us do our jobs then we'll help you with what you need. Promise."

Mia's shoulders slumped. She inhaled a deep breath and let it out slowly as her eyes moved from Creed to his.

"Okay."

Caiden finished his perusal and highlighting in his intel as to Nadia Petrov and uploaded it. He then told Creed so he knew what was happening. Then, without missing a beat, he began doing some research on Dominick Nelson and Ashton Stewart, Mia's brother. He'd known her as Mia Stewart back home. Before she changed her name.

He started searching in the Smoky Ridge newspaper archives for any mention of Dominick Nelson. Then he logged into the Federal Prison Systems to search for Dominick. Once he ruled out these sources he'd log into the RAPTOR search system and search all other mentions of Dominick Nelson, beginning with state and local jail records, arrests, addresses, and real estate searches. He'd find Nelson, if he existed and if he was still alive. Two ifs, he hoped he could lay to rest soon. The thought that Mia was a murderer was sickening to him, but he had to rest his suspicion, and also be sure that he and his teammates weren't wasting time on someone they should be having arrested. Even if it was someone he cared about.

His computer screen populated and he eagerly read the results. Nelson did indeed exist and had been arrested many times. Though he'd always managed to avoid jail, there were any number of infractions against him. Solicitation. Drug use. Possession with the intent to sell. Battery. Bar fights. Then an article popped up that grabbed his attention. The headline read: "Smoky Ridge resident arrested for solicitation to deliver illegal packages." The newspaper was careful not to imply drugs.

As he read the full article his heart began to race. Nelson had been accused by a young girl, name withheld, of forcing her to deliver packages for him. When asked how she was forced, she said he'd threatened to kill her if she didn't do as he said. The girl stated that another girl she knew had been beaten up as she walked home from school. But after delivering a few more packages, the girl told her father what was happening, and the father took her to the police station where she'd confessed to making deliveries for Nelson. But she didn't have any proof. The victim then left town, out of fear for her life, to live with an aunt in another state. He looked at the date of the article. It was written two years ago.

Caiden glanced at Mia, who continued to pour over her notes, oblivious to the fact that he was sweating, and his hands shook as he read the report. She'd been telling the truth, at least about the packages.

Caiden swallowed a dry lump in his throat. "Mia."

When her beautiful brown eyes met his, he licked his lips. "He's still doing it. Nelson. He's still delivering his drugs via young messengers."

Her eyes glistened and his heart cracked a bit at the sadness in her eyes. Brushing her hand on the leg of her jeans she swallowed, "How do you know?" Her bottom lip trembled slightly, and a lone tear silently slid down her soft cheek. He watched the moisture leave a trail down to her jaw where it continued under her jaw. Mia swiped it away and sniffed softly.

"I found a newspaper article from two years ago. The story sounds just like yours."

"Oh my God, I was scared and ran. But now, other girls' lives are ruined because I ran instead of going to the police."

"You had no way of knowing what would happen."

14

As she read the words, she had to stop and swipe the moisture from her eyes so she could see. It sure sounded like her story, except this lucky girl's mother was still alive. The article went on further to say that she most likely left town because after she'd gone to police, ugly stories began to circulate around school that she was a whore and slept with dozens of guys. She was a druggy. She was trouble and looking for attention. Her friends stopped talking to her and she was ashamed and left town.

"He did that to her." Mia said to no one in particular.

Caiden rubbed her back as she sat next to him, her nose still running slightly, tears still threatening to spill over her cheeks. "Did what to her?"

"Spread the rumors. Made her life a hell. Discredited her so no one would believe her. It's sickening."

"Yes, it's how these people operate. They're breaking the law, but they throw shade on innocent people to make themselves shine in the sun."

"It's disgusting."

"It is. I agree."

Mia sat up straighter, then brushed the moisture from her cheeks before standing up and wrapping her arms around her waist. Her mind reeled with all that had gone on while she'd been gone. Sure, she was a kid and immature. And scared as shit. All she could think of was to get the hell out of there before Nelson killed her just like he'd killed her mom. She did nothing to stop him.

"I feel like I've been given this chance. I feel like I have to do something Caiden. I have to right some of the wrongs I've created."

Caiden set his computer on the bed and walked to her. His arms slowly wrapped around her and pulled her into his body. His warmth mixed with the strength of his body and his fresh scent made her feel safe. Oh what she would have given to feel his arms around her all those years ago. All the years since. She hadn't felt safe a single day since she'd left Smoky Ridge sixteen years ago.

"You couldn't have known what would happen. All you knew at the time was your father was gone. Your brother was away at college and your mother had been murdered in front of you."

She allowed herself to believe that was true for a few moments. "What did you think? When I left, what did you believe about me?"

She felt his throat move as he swallowed, heard his heartbeat increase, and she closed her eyes as she waited for him to respond. His breathing shook his chest and for the first time she could hear how hard it was for him to breathe. As she nestled her head against his chest, she listened to his lungs work hard, and her heart hurt for Caiden too.

"I thought you were dead."

Her arms snaked around his waist as she pulled him close, relieved when he tightened his arms around her instead of pulling away. She held her breath, trying to stave off the burst of tears that threatened. She'd let them flow later tonight as she lay in bed. Until then she was going to do whatever she could to help Caiden and Creed. Then, she'd screw up the courage to face Dominick Nelson and stop him from corrupting any more young people.

Caiden's arms squeezed her once again, then he released her and she felt his loss immediately. He stepped back and cleared his throat.

"Okay. So, we know Nelson is still operating and we know it's likely larger than we can imagine. I've found police records, arrest records, drug arrests, etc. So let's see what else I can find out. Creed and I need to finish our mission here in Vegas. Then, you and I will go back home to Smoky Ridge and clear your name."

"Is my brother still alive?"

"He's next on my list."

She nodded, and her eyes landed on Creed, who sat in his chair watching them, a smile on his face. She smiled in return, then sat on her bench and resumed looking for anything she thought would help them.

Caiden picked up her phone and looked at it. "We're meeting our secret texter at seven tonight behind the Stardust Casino."

Creed nodded. "Looks like I'm headed out to the Stardust for some recon."

Caiden offered, "I'll go with you."

"No, you stay here and keep searching for more names we can investigate and any other clues that may be of use. Dildo saw you and probably assumes you're now after him. I'll go and look like a tourist."

Creed walked to the bathroom he shared with Caiden, and she heard the rustling of clothing. He reappeared in a couple of minutes wearing an Hawaiian shirt, a baseball cap, and khakis. Mia's brows furrowed together.

"Isn't that going to make you stand out?"

"Perhaps. But that's the plan. When I scope out where I need to go to see the back of the building, I can remove the loud shirt and switch out my baseball cap for a stocking hat." He pulled one from a duffle on the floor. "Then I look totally different."

"Wow." Her limited vocabulary at the moment irritated her but really what could you say to stuff like that? These guys were impressive.

Caiden tapped on her phone a few times, then handed her phone back. "Don't respond to him anymore today Mia. Just before meeting time I'll ask you to make contact, but now it's radio silence. We want to keep him on edge wondering if you'll follow through or not."

"Okay." She glanced at the text he'd sent to her texter. "I'll be there."

15

Creed left to do his recon and Caiden took a moment to gather himself. He walked to the bathroom and turned on the water faucet, splashed water on his face, then over his hands. He pulled a towel off the holder and dried his face, then sat on the closed toilet and put his head in his hands. His heartbeat was erratic and he was emotional. So many things to grapple with right now and he didn't want to screw up. It was important to him and his teammates that he do his job well. It was equally important to him to help Mia. He still had those feelings he'd had back in the day. They were different now, mature feelings, but they were now mixed with fear that she'd run again. And that she'd not told him the whole truth.

Inhaling as deeply as he could, he released the air from his lungs slowly, then stood and left the bathroom. Mia still sat on her bench, looking over her notes and he decided to access the autopsy report on her mom's death.

It should certainly help him, at a minimum, rule Mia out as the murderer.

He pushed the guilty feeling down as he typed into the computer network at RAPTOR to access the records he could. They often accessed autopsy records as they investigated, so this shouldn't raise any eyes with the authorities they worked through. And, if it did, he'd need to tell someone what was in the works and hope they'd offer assistance if needed. Since Nelson had a long rap sheet, they'd be looking for police help soon enough. But right now, he'd put all the puzzle pieces in place and hope for the best. Worrying about it without doing everything he could, was a waste of time.

After he typed in the search parameters, he went back to the reports on Nadia Petrov and continued searching for any other existence of her.

"Mia, in your notes is there any mention of Anton Smith, Jerard Maddox, or Michael Summers?"

"Not in my notes, but on my recorder, I have the last interview I conducted with Nikita. I didn't have the time to transcribe the recording yet. I was going to do that today."

"Do you recall why they were mentioned?"

Mia cocked her head slightly and stared into his eyes. "Nikita said she overheard two men mention Mik-ha-il Summers was coming to approve of them. She must have meant Michael. Her English is very broken."

"So I'll add Michael Summers to my search parameters as someone who may have traveled back and forth between here and Russia."

He began typing, excitement once again surging through his veins. He'd focus on this for the time being and do a great job. It was in all of their blood to stop these guys, especially Dildo.

"Caiden, will you go with me to my office to get my recorder? I have more notes on there that may be important."

He stopped typing and looked into her eyes. He'd always loved looking into her eyes. They were a beautiful dark brown instead they shined.

"Let's talk about it when Creed gets back. Once he's done with his recon, we may know a bit more of what we're dealing with. I suspect we're going to be calling in some back up here so that'll give us a bit more flexibility in moving around the city."

His computer chimed and he looked at the email he received. The autopsy on Mia's mother from the West Virginia Medical Examiner's Office.

Mia responded softly, "Okay."

He barely heard her over the loud beating of his heart. He clicked on the report and read the basics. Her throat had been slashed, the wound started below her right ear and sliced around then up at an angle consistent with someone of around six feet in height and left handed. He let out a breath, it wasn't Mia. He then went back to the jail records of Dominick Nelson and saw that his height was registered at six foot one and he was left-handed. It could easily be him.

He looked at Mia and as if she could feel him looking at her she lifted her head. "Mia, I pulled your mom's autopsy report."

She gasped and her shoulders stiffened. "Why?"

"Because we need to compile a profile of her killer. I mean, the police already have a profile, but I want to match similarities with Nelson so when we go to Smoky Ridge, we can show them the similarities of her killer with Nelson. Then with you as an eyewitness, we should be able to get a conviction."

"We can't do that unless we know Ashton is alive and safe. Nelson will target him."

"We'll be careful about how we approach it. I promise."

Mia set her records aside and leaned back against the wall. Her eyes bored into his. "Did you look up my mom's autopsy report to make sure it wasn't me who killed her?"

Caiden's throat constricted and dried and he had to work to swallow through the narrow opening. "Partly."

Her nose wrinkled and she closed her eyes. He worried about her next reaction but admitted to himself he'd be pissed if the tables were turned. When she opened her eyes though, she huffed out a breath and said, "Thank you for being honest with me."

"I'm sorry Mia. In my line of work, I don't take a person's word for anything. I research everything."

"I understand." She tucked a lock of hair behind her ear, and he noticed that her fingers shook. "I don't like how it makes me feel, but I do understand it."

He relaxed slightly and set his computer aside. He moved to sit beside Mia on her bench and folded his hands around hers. “I’m sorry. We have to learn to trust each other again. I’m still reeling a bit at finding you. Then learning your story. It’s a lot to take in in a few hours.”

16

Mia stared at their clasped hands, his tan, hers pale. His larger, hers not. His rougher, her hands were smooth. His hands were warm, hers were cool. They were opposites all around. Except they both stayed in the shadows when they could. Caiden to save women and children who'd been wrongfully taken and forced into a life they didn't deserve. She out of fear for her life. But she understood living on the fringes of life. She understood his desire to save innocents from the assholes of society. She wanted to do that too.

"I know what you mean. It's been a lot for me to take in today as well. It was a shock seeing you again."

"I guess I have the advantage over you there. I knew a couple of weeks ago that you were still alive. I wrestled with myself over contacting you or not. In the end, I just couldn't let you go again without seeing you and talking to you. I needed to find out what had happened."

She finally looked into his eyes. "I'm glad you did."

Caiden swallowed, licked his lips then leaned in, but stopped just shy of her mouth. Mia raised her left hand to cup his right cheek. She swayed in and kissed his lips lightly.

It was electric. She felt it throughout her whole body as his tongue sought entry past her lips and she opened them further, needing to feel his kiss once again.

He tilted his head slightly and she followed his lead. Their lips fit together perfectly. Soft, wet, slow. His kiss sent jolts of excitement through her body. Her nipples puckered tightly, and her blood flow pulsed between her legs, and sent chills down her arms and legs.

Her breathing grew shallow and when his hand pressed against the back of her head and held her in place, a moan escaped, and he deepened his kiss. It was everything she remembered and more. It was overwhelming, beautiful, and sexy.

Time had stood still for her. The past sixteen years of wondering, yearning, reliving their time together. It had been held in a closed part of her, tucked away safely to bring out only when she felt strong enough to remember it. But now, Caiden was here, in the flesh and the damn had a crack in it and was about to burst open.

He tugged at her blouse; she pulled at his t-shirt. Her skin grew warm.

"I want you," she whispered against his lips.

He pulled away and looked into her eyes. "Are you sure?"

"Yes."

He took her hand and pulled her to her feet, walked them through the adjoining door to her room and closed the door behind them. She pulled her blouse off and he twisted the lock on the door. His eyes roamed down her body, slowly as she unzipped her pants and pulled them down her hips.

"You're simply gorgeous."

A blush warmed her cheeks. "You're as handsome as ever."

Caiden closed the distance between them in a split second. His shirt came off as her shaking fingers unfastened his jeans and lowered the zipper. His thickened cock jutted forward, and she rubbed the back of her fingers against it which made him groan. His hands cupped her breasts and squeezed them just enough to make her pant, then slid around to her back and unhooked her bra. He pulled her bra free and rubbed his calloused thumbs over her taut nipples. The roughness caused a flash of moisture to gather between her legs and her eyes flew open. Her breathing was rough, ragged, and came in spurts, the flood of emotions was overwhelming.

He smiled then, "Are you wet for me, Baby?"

She whispered, "Yes."

He shook his head slightly, "I love hearing that."

His fingers roamed down her torso and pulled her panties over her hips, letting them fall to the floor. His fingers quickly replaced her panties, his fingers massaging between her lips until he found her clit and added pressure. She couldn't stop the gasp that escaped, and he kissed her once again, his lips claiming hers so possessively that she never wanted it to end. She belonged right here with Caiden. It had always been him. Her first time, second time, third time and now, it was Caiden.

He quickly pulled away only far enough to bend and lift her into his arms and carry her to the bed. His knee rested on the bed as he leaned over and gently lay her in the middle. He never looked away from her as he finished taking his clothes off and she couldn't look away from him either. He was simply beautiful. He had defined muscles that bunched and stretched under the smooth tanned skin of his torso. As he bent to remove his jeans, he was graceful and sure. Instead of standing once again so she could admire him further, he slowly kissed his way up her left leg, then his lips encased her clit and sucked while at the same time flicking his tongue and she nearly exploded. She'd waited sixteen years for Caiden's touch. Though she never let herself believe she'd feel it again.

All too soon he kissed his way up her torso, laving each nipple with his tongue first, then his lips were once again on hers.

She felt the tip of his cock at her entrance but all she saw was the blue of his eyes holding hers captive. He pushed himself into her, slowly, savoring every feeling that came over him. She could see it in his face as he tried controlling his reactions. She didn't care enough to control her reaction, she let out a long slow moan as he filled her, and her hands wrapped around his waist as much as she could as he held himself slightly above her. He pulled out slowly and slid back in and it felt just as good as the first time. When she opened her eyes, his were watching her and she couldn't look away. He mesmerized her as he pulled out and pushed back in. Out and in, slowly the rhythm started, then he sped up as she cried out, "I'm so close."

He pushed in harder and faster now, each of them had labored breathing as they sought to find their release. Caiden's hips rotated against her as he pushed in, then he pulled out and do it again. Her body warmed, her skin dampened, and finally she felt the white-hot release she'd needed for the past sixteen years. Caiden pumped into her a few more times, then groaned loudly as his release rolled over him.

17

Caiden rested his elbows on either side of Mia's head, his right cheek rested against hers. He waited for his breathing to regulate, then he slowly pulled himself from her warmth, rolled over, and pulled a tissue from the box on the bedside table. He removed the condom he'd put on prior to entering Mia and tossed it in the trash can.

"When did you put that on?"

He smiled at her lazy words. "Just before I slid inside of you."

"I didn't see that."

"You were enjoying my tongue."

Her lips curved into a sweet smile and he enjoyed watching this new Mia, relaxed and satisfied.

"You've gotten very good at donning a condom. I won't ask how you've practiced. I'm not sure I'd like the answer."

He lay on the bed beside her, enjoying her nakedness and not feeling a bit shy about it. "Don't tell me you haven't had boyfriends over the years."

She looked at him, her expression showing sadness and maybe shyness. "Mia, tell me."

A single tear slid from her eye and he immediately hated the direction of this conversation. Using the back of his fingers he brushed the tear from her temple, then gently turned her face to his. "No one?"

She pinched her lips together but said nothing.

"Why?"

Mia huffed out a breath and sat up. She reached down and picked up her blouse and slid her arms inside. "I didn't trust anyone. I couldn't trust anyone. I never knew how Dominick would get to me and I feared he'd pay someone to befriend me and get me in a vulnerable situation then turn on me."

Caiden sat up and pulled Mia onto his lap. He cradled her gently and kissed her temple. Eventually she relaxed and he enjoyed holding her for a while longer. This poor woman had been so scared that she'd avoided intimate relationships for sixteen years. How lonely she must have been. It broke his heart to think of her lonely and afraid. It also sealed his resolve to help her. If he could help it at all, she'd never be afraid and lonely again.

He kissed her temple again. "I'm sorry, Baby. I'm so sorry."

Taking a deep breath, Mia then kissed him softly and stood. "I'm going to take a shower."

"Okay. I'm going to my room and do the same, all my stuff is there. I'll close the door, but open it when you've finished and we'll keep working until Creed gets back with his plan for tonight."

"Okay."

He watched as she padded across the carpeted floor to the bathroom, gathering her clothing along the way. With a huff of a breath he gathered his clothes and went to shower.

As he closed the door behind him, he heard Creed scan his card and he hustled to the bathroom and closed the door. He made quick work of a shower, eager to speak with Creed about their plan.

When he opened the bathroom door he was disappointed to see Mia's door still closed.

Creed looked up from his phone as he lay on his bed. "I took pictures of the area."

"You didn't see anyone lurking around doing recon on our recon?"

Creed laughed, "No, jackwad, I didn't."

"I didn't mean to insult you. I just thought that's what he was playing at by giving us several hours before the meeting."

"I think it'll be dark by then. At least behind the Stardust it will. It's blocked in, which is interesting. Buildings all around it. An alley going in and out, no dumpsters, nothing to hide behind and no windows, or few windows looking out on that area. The only thing there, is a picnic table where the staff seems to take their breaks."

Caiden looked at Creed's pictures, his brows furrowed as he wondered what Dildo, or whoever, was up to. "Even the other buildings don't have doors leading out to this area, just the Stardust."

"Right. So, I'm wondering if he has an in at the Stardust. An employee who is a friend, or he's staying there, or some other familiarity with the casino."

Caiden pulled his phone from his pocket and dialed Deacon at headquarters.

"What's up? You staying in Vegas forever?"

"No! Although it is nice here."

"Shut up. We've already lost Pipes to Vegas, we can't lose you too."

"Nah, I'm wondering if you can hack into the employee database at the Stardust Casino and Hotel here in Vegas and see if anyone jumps out at you. Also the guest manifest. Looking for Dildo specifically. But also one of our other persons of interest. They're trying to set up a meeting there tonight with Mia."

"You're not letting her go, are you?"

"No, I'm still working out what we're going to do."

"Piper's back from her honeymoon, send her in."

"That's a great idea. You get to hacking, I'll call Piper."

"Ten-four."

Caiden looked at Creed and smiled. "Piper's back from her honeymoon. What do you think about sticking a dark wig on her and sending her in to meet Dildo?"

"That's fantastic. You and I can be watching from the corners of the building."

Caiden dialed Piper's phone just as Mia walked into the room smelling fresh and looking rested and relaxed. He winked at her and she smiled.

Piper answered, "Hi Caiden, what's up?"

"Hey Pipes. Are you up for a recon mission tonight? We're hoping to capture Dildo."

"Finally! Absolutely I'm in. When and where?"

"I'll text you the deets. We can meet at the hotel and go over them together. Bring a long black wig, you'll need to look like Mia."

"Dildo wants to meet Mia?"

"Fucker's been texting threats to her."

"No way? Why?"

"I don't know other than he's pissed about her story on the girls and mentioning his name."

Caiden looked towards Mia as he spoke and could tell she was growing uncomfortable with the conversation.

"Hey Pipes, be here at the hotel around six tonight."

He ended the conversation and dropped his phone into his pocket; he walked to Mia and inhaled the fresh aroma. "You alright?"

“I don’t like how this is all playing out.”

“It’s our job, honey.”

“This is how Sherry, one of the American girls, was kidnapped. Piper was kidnapped once; you can’t make her go through that again. Not because of me.”

18

Caiden's face was marred by the worry lines between his brows. She'd always been fascinated by those lines on his handsome face. It was how she knew when he was worried or frustrated.

"What do you mean that's how Sherry was kidnapped?"

Mia bent to pick her notes up off the bench she'd sat on just an hour ago. Flipping through the pages, she found the section reserved for Sherry; she'd separated her notebook into sections so she could keep their notes straight, because the women would remember things later and call her. Scanning Sherry's notes, Mia found the story of Sherry's kidnapping.

"It says here, 'She called me and said she was suicidal and needed to talk. She told me she and I both went to college at the University of Nevada. She got my name from a help list at school. She said she was embarrassed and anxious and didn't want to be seen in public. So I went to a restaurant she said she worked at, Benedict's Cafe And Coffee

House. She said she takes her breaks at seven. I got there and the last thing I remember is feeling a prick in my neck and a woman looking at someone behind me and smiling.'"

Caiden looked at the notes then at her. "So we're looking for a woman?"

"I don't think so. I think they hired someone to lure her there, who wouldn't be threatening. For some reason Sherry felt like the woman she saw was getting paid to call her and lure her there. She felt that way because there was a back door to the restaurant, but the woman didn't walk out from it, she entered the alley from the street."

Creed scooted to the foot of the bed. "We don't know who this is that's texting. It could be Dildo but by texting we don't know."

"But he's not trying to be nice, he's been menacing." Mia added.

Caiden turned to her. "Then we'll be menacing right back."

"What do you mean?"

Caiden glanced at Creed, who nodded at him. He turned again to Mia. "Baby, give me your phone."

She swallowed the fear that threatened her stomach. Slowly she held her phone out to him. She trusted him, but it was difficult for her to see how they'd come out of this without anyone getting hurt.

Caiden tapped out a message on her phone, then hit send. When his eyes met hers, she stared at him and hoped he knew what he was doing.

"I've established that you aren't just going to go along. I told him if he wants your notes from the Container World article, he'll meet when and where you say."

Her phone chimed, and Caiden looked down at it and grinned. "He's not happy."

Caiden then turned to her. "We'll get you a new phone and number to use while we're monopolizing your phone Mia."

Her fingers began to shake. She felt like she was losing all control here and that couldn't happen. "Caiden, I don't want a new phone or phone number. This is all making me feel panicky. I've spent most of my life protecting myself and maintaining control over my life. I can't, and by that I mean I won't, just blithely hand it over to you or anyone else. So, you and Creed..." She glanced briefly at Creed to make sure he was listening. "Need to start letting me in and big time. I've been through enough in my life. I will not sit on the sidelines and hope my big strong protector will save me. I'm my own protector."

Creed laughed. "There you go, Mia. You've got spunk, I'll say that."

Caiden's brows furrowed and the crease between his brows grew deeper. He ran his hands down his face and took a deep breath.

He handed her phone back and nodded. "I'm sorry, Mia. I didn't mean to make you feel anxious or scared. But for the record, I will do everything in my power to protect you."

Mia smiled. "There are worse things a woman can have than a protector. As long as he knows she's strong and will also protect herself."

Caiden stepped to her and hugged her fully. She could feel his body shake and his breathing came in spurts. She hugged him back, trying without words to reassure him. And in all honesty, she wasn't sure what she'd do, but she knew she wasn't going to sit in a hotel room and wait for life to play itself out around her.

When Caiden stepped back he took a deep breath and said, "Okay. Let's plan out what we're going to do."

Before any discussion took place, Mia's phone chimed again and she stepped close to Caiden and read the message.

The name on the message was Vika. "They're tracking us. It's why they let us keep our phones."

She immediately called Vika.

"Yes. It's Vika."

"Vika, it's Mia. Where are you? How do you know they're tracking you?"

"I saw him. The mean one."

"Who is that? Who is the mean one?"

She looked at Caiden who was stone still waiting to hear, so she tapped the speaker icon so he and Creed could hear Vika.

"The one that hit Eleese."

"Dilano?"

"Yes. What did Piper call him? Dildo?"

"Where are you and where did you see him?"

"We are all in a house. Close to airport. After investigation we go home."

"Vika, did you call the police?"

"They said nothing they can do if he didn't hurt us."

"Is Dilano there now?"

"No, he left. But, he'll be back. He was here in the morning."

"Okay. He was there this morning? Is that the first time you saw him?"

"Yes."

"Okay, Vika, you call me right away if you see him again. I am here with RAPTOR and they want to capture Dilano. They'll help you."

"Yes. Yes. Thank you."

"Don't leave the house Vika. Stay there and keep the doors locked."

"Yes. I understand."

Mia looked at Caiden. "It all makes a bit more sense now. They let them keep their phones because they've put trackers on them. They can find them if they go missing."

Caiden looked at Creed then her. "I think we need to send Piper in as Mia, she can stay with the girls and check their phones for tracking devices and what they are. Pipes can upload the information from the tracking devices to our system and we can turn it around and track them."

Creed stood. "That's brilliant."

"Why can't I go in? I know these women."

19

Caiden ran a wire up the back of Mia's blouse giving her directions as he did. "This will keep us in contact at all times." He wove the wire through the back of her hair, which was pulled back in a ponytail. Then hooked the wire to an earpiece and asked her to fit it into her ear. "It's virtually invisible but necessary in case their tracking devices also contain audio. Don't tell anyone you have this on. Just make sure you explain everything you're doing as you do it and who you are talking to."

"Okay."

She glanced over at Piper, who was also setting up a communication device, exactly like hers. Piper wore a dark wig, pulled back into a ponytail matching hers. They were to go in, one at a time, Piper watching the area and sending Mia in first, then Piper would go in the back door with Mia's assistance. They had note pads and pens with them to write notes to the Russian women, so they didn't say anything to alert Dildo they were on to their tracking units.

Piper finished with her comm unit, then picked up her laptop case and looked at her and smiled. "Ready?"

"Yeah."

"Okay, let's go."

The four of them left the hotel room and split up into two vehicles. Piper had her black SUV and Caiden and Creed jumped into a similar looking rental.

Piper pulled out of the parking garage first, and they merged into traffic on the street. Piper navigated expertly as they made their way from the hotel district and toward the area of residences close to the airport.

"Piper, how do you know which house they're at?"

"We contacted the police department and they told us where their safe house is. When we explained it wasn't so safe right now, they seemed a bit sheepish but, PDs are so understaffed and under pressure these days. I'm just glad we're here to help them."

"Me too."

Piper navigated the gates at the entrance to the neighborhood and slowed the SUV down to under twenty miles per hour. Her head turned back and forth as she looked at each house. When she caught Mia's gaze, she smiled. "I'm looking for activity. General neighborhood behaviors such as all garage doors down or open doors or people walking. I see three women walking up ahead, they feel safe. I see kids playing in yards and I see swing sets in backyards. So a safe upper- middle-class neighborhood.

She turned onto a street and slowed, then pulled to the curb.

"That's the house across the street. The yellow house with white trim. What's different about that house from the others?"

Mia looked at the house. "No swing set in the backyard. All the lights are on in the house while the rest of the houses are still dark or only have one room lit. Even though it's still early dusk. All the shades are pulled down while most of the other homes have their shades pulled up. The garage door is closed."

"Excellent Mia." Piper nodded. "Call Vika and ask her to open the garage door with the opener inside. I'll pull my car in the garage."

Mia tapped Vika's number and smiled when Vika answered before the second ring.

"Mia?"

"Yes Vika, it's me. Please open the garage door for us."

"You are here?"

"Yes."

"It's safe?"

"Right now it is and we're here to make it safer."

"Yes. Okay."

Both she and Piper watched as the garage door opened and Piper backed her SUV up the driveway and into the garage. After they exited the SUV Piper tapped the button on the wall by the door and closed the door. They both entered the house feeling confident they'd not been seen.

Mia quickly wrote on a sheet of paper: "I need your phones. Please don't talk about it, just hand them over. We're looking for the tracking devices."

Handing the note to Vika, Mia watched as she read the note. Vika looked at her and nodded, then pulled her phone from her back pocket and handed her phone to Mia. Nodding, Mia handed it to Piper who had set up her computer on the kitchen table.

Piper plugged the phone into the computer and tapped a few keys. Mia took the note around the house to the other women and gathered their phones. One by one Piper plugged them in and found the software trackers added to each of their phones. They were hidden in a games app and virtually undetected, unless you knew what you were doing.

Piper pulled burner phones from her laptop case and nodded to Mia. Mia began opening all of the packages of phones and Piper plugged them in and reloaded the tracking software into the burner phone.

"Mia, there's no audio on these tracking devices, it's all tracking only."

Mia let out a breath and looked at the women, who all stood along the wall in the kitchen watching what was happening, fear on their faces.

Natalia was the first to say something. "I want that bastard dead."

The other women nodded. "We go home now."

Natalia walked into the living room and peeked through the blinds to the street. She turned and looked at Mia and shook her head no.

Piper then updated Caiden and Creed. "No audio, I'm sure you heard. Tracking devices have all been uploaded into burner phones."

"Ten-four. Caiden is coming in to grab the burners."

Mia went to the back door and let Caiden inside. He kissed her forehead then walked to the kitchen table and put all the burner phones into a backpack.

"We're taking these burners with the tracking devices and we'll drop them off all over town. You need to turn off all the lights in the house and stay out of sight. They'll send someone here to see if you're actually gone when they see the phones on the move."

Mia nodded, "Okay. We'll take care of things here."

Caiden left and Piper handed the women their phones back. "Your phones are clean now. No tracking on them."

Natalia nodded then she and Vika exchanged words in Russian. Soon the women went into the rooms and turned the lights off. They made their way back to the living room and huddled together on the sofa and chairs.

Natalia addressed Mia. "We don't like dark. Too much dark when we come here."

The containers had been dark. It frightened them so much they were all now afraid of the dark. Mia's heart hurt for them.

20

Caiden listened to Mia work with the women. She was strong, spoke softly but succinctly and got the job done. Now it was up to him and Creed to disburse the tracked burners and hopefully lure out Dildo and whoever else he might be working with.

He left the house with the phones and jumped into the SUV. Creed took off as soon as he was in the vehicle and he glanced back to make sure the lights were being turned off at the house. He saw them going out one by one.

Creed looked over at him, "Where do you want to drop off the first phone?"

"Let's take them into the casinos on the strip and tuck them in hiding places so it'll take them a while to find them."

"Roger that. Emmy has help coming back to us. Diego and Falcon, I believe."

"That works out great. We'll have them stationed where they can watch these phones we're hiding. Let's hide them in twos."

Creed navigated Vegas traffic perfectly and they split up once they were on the strip. He took the Paris and Bally's. Creed took the Bellagio and Caesar's Palace.

Caiden started at the Paris. The instant he entered, the noise level rose an octave with the chattering of people, and the chimes and bells of the games being played. The overpowering odor of cigarette smoke assaulted his nostrils, and he pulled the neckline of his t-shirt up over his nose.

He walked through the casino, around the slot machines. He pulled some coins from his pocket and dropped them in a slot machine and watched as the cherries, oranges, and lemons spun inside. He took the time to check the bottom of the machine and saw a narrow space just under the machine. He pulled two burners from his pocket and slid them under the machine and pushed them back. He pulled the lever a couple more times then stood and walked out of the casino and headed over to Bally's to do the same thing there.

He told his team members, "I've hidden the first two phones in Paris under slot number 456."

Creed responded, "I've hidden two phones under slot number 243 in the Bellagio."

It took him a while to navigate the sidewalk and tourists milling about the Vegas strip, but he managed to enter Bally's just as Creed said, "I've hidden two phones in Caesar's Palace on a shelf at roulette table number eight."

"Nice move," Caiden responded and headed toward the roulette tables. As he approached them, he noticed the detailed carvings and angles on the outside of the table, and figured he'd see if he could hide a phone there. Pleased when a phone dropped into a space on the table he dropped the next one in, stood and watched the table's game for a bit then turned and left Bally's. "Last two phones in Bally's at roulette table number five."

Caiden waited until he was on the sidewalk before asking, "Mia and Piper. How are things at the house?"

Mia spoke first, "Good, but we're watching an SUV driving by very slowly on its second pass."

"They've noticed that the phones have moved. Stay hidden."

"Okay." Her voice sounded breathless and he worried about her level of fear and reliving her past during this time.

"Mia. If you need anything, let me know immediately."

"I will."

Piper responded, "She's doing great Caid. We're good."

"Thanks Pipes."

He entered the hotel he and Creed were staying at and waited at the door. "Creed, I'm at the hotel. Are you close?"

"Just pulling up now. Jump in."

Caiden made tracks to the SUV and jumped in. As soon as his door was closed, Creed eased them out into traffic and on the road back to the house. Caiden couldn't escape the feeling that something was off, and he squeezed his hands together tightly to stave off the paranoia.

As Creed drove them toward the neighborhood where the women were located, he heard glass shattering and screams over their comm units.

"Mia?" No answer.

Creed stepped on the gas to get them closer. Gun shots sounded over the comm units and Caiden held his breath.

Then Piper hissed, "Shit. Shit. Shit."

"Pipes, what's happening?"

"Someone tried breaking into the house. I shot and got him in the arm. It wasn't Dildo. He took off running and I didn't have a good shot to drop him."

"Is everyone alright?"

"Yes, just scared."

He heard one of the women yell, "We go home now."

Their visit to the US certainly wasn't a good one. Creed turned into the subdivision then onto the street.

"Mia and Piper, we're almost there. Don't shoot at us. We'll pull in the driveway."

"Roger." Piper responded.

"Mia, are you alright?"

He heard her heavy breathing and his stomach twisted. Finally she responded. "Yes. I'm alright."

Creed pulled into the driveway and said, "We just pulled in the driveway. We're coming to the front door. Let us in."

They jumped from the SUV and ran to the front of the house. The door jerked open just as they landed on the front step. Piper smiled as she saw them and flipped the light switch on so they could see. Caiden looked around and saw Mia sitting on the sofa, her skin had paled and her lips were trembling but she had her arm around one of the Russian women; he thought it was Misha.

He hurried to her and she jumped up and threw her arms around him, her trembling body clung to him tightly.

"It's alright baby, I'm here."

"Caiden." Her words were broken by sobs. "I was so scared. It came rushing back to me. I saw my mom's scared eyes."

His arms wrapped around her tightly, "It's okay. I'm here and I won't let anything happen to you."

"I want to be brave."

"Oh honey, you are brave."

21

He held her and silently vowed he'd never let her go again.

Creed softly said, "Police are on their way."

"Thanks Creed."

He whispered in Mia's ear. "Baby, when we're finished speaking with the police, we're going back to the hotel and buckling down for the night. Then, when you're ready, we're going to have a chat, just you and me. Okay?"

She lightly sniffed, then nodded her head against his. "Okay."

Sirens wailed outside and he rubbed her back then loosened his hold on her. He looked into her eyes. "Okay?"

She tried to smile, but it was the effort that mattered. "Okay."

Police squads stopped in front of the house and officers came to the door. Piper took over explaining what had happened while he and Creed were gone. Mia had to answer questions and she then sat with the Russian women as they explained their stories, helping with translation where she could. He and Creed were simply there for moral support.

Caiden texted Emmy and told her what went down. "Do you want us to explain that we pulled tracking info off their phones?"

Emmy responded quickly. "Let me call their chief and smooth things over."

"Roger."

He stood by and waited until he could bring Mia back to the hotel. But he watched her to make sure she was emotionally alright. She seemed to have gotten the worst of her emotions under check, but he would make sure she was okay later. If she needed to see a counselor, he'd help her with that also. Whatever she needed.

Creed came to stand by him and softly said, "Diego and Falcon have landed and are on their way to watch two locations. If you want to stay with Mia, Pipes and I can go watch the other two locations."

He turned to Creed, relief filled his chest. "I appreciate that Creed. I'd like to stay and make sure she's alright."

Creed smiled at him. "It's good to see you in love, man. You seem less crabby."

"I didn't say I was in love."

"See, when you're in love it shows, and you don't have to say it." Creed shrugged and went to chat with Piper. Piper looked over at Caid and smiled. She said good-bye to Mia and left with Creed, who tossed him the keys to the SUV on their way out.

Caiden studied Mia, who sat quietly next to Natalia as she spoke to a police officer. Mia looked up at him and smiled. He stared, likely longer than he should, but he had always loved looking at her. To him, she was the most beautiful woman he'd ever laid eyes on.

It took a couple of hours before the women were packed up, loaded onto a bus, and taken to another safe house where they'd have constant police protection with them. That was only decided after Emmy called their chief and explained what they were dealing with.

The women were grateful for the help. They promised to keep in touch with Mia and let her know if they remembered anything she should know to help them stop Dildo and his group.

Caiden wrapped his arm around Mia's shoulders and walked her to the SUV, got her in the passenger seat and buckled in, then climbed in himself. He felt exhausted suddenly and realized all that had happened today.

As he navigated the traffic, he glanced at Mia often but said nothing.

"I'm not going to break. I had a scare today, a couple of them, and my nerves got jumbled together. But, I'm fine. And I got more information. One of the names you need to be looking for is Jasper Mitchell. He works with Dildo to procure women. Apparently he was the driver Dildo, Dawson, and Haywood were waiting for with the American women."

"Nice work Mia. We may make an operative out of you."

She chuckled. "No thanks. I'll stick with reporting. But I can tell you this, my stories are going to get a lot more gritty and real time. And now I have more confidence to tell stories as they are, not whitewashed to reassure people. Women need to be scared. This shit is happening all the time and it needs to be stopped."

He smiled and nodded his head. "There you are. I've been waiting for the passionate and determined Mia I used to know to make her appearance. I'm glad your fighting spirit is coming back to you, baby."

"My fighting spirit has always been with me, Caid. It was just busy hiding me and keeping me alive. Now though, I'm ready to get in the dirt and really fight." She twisted slightly in her seat. "It's because of you. I feel safe for the first time in my life and it's because of you."

His vision wavered in front of him as his eyes filled with tears. "I'll do everything in my power to protect you Mia. Forever and always."

She whispered. "Forever and always." Mia swiped a tear from her cheek. "I'll do everything in my power to keep you with me Caiden. Forever and always."

He swallowed the lump in his throat and turned into the parking garage. He found a space quickly and made his way around the truck in record time. He whipped open the passenger door and Mia lunged out at him. Her arms around his shoulders and her lips on his as he pulled her body close and held her tightly. He enjoyed her lips, the feel of her body pressed to his, the way she smelled. All of her.

Footsteps approached and he set her on the ground and stood in front of her, ever the protector. A man walked past them snickering.

Caiden closed the passenger door and locked the SUV, then took Mia's hand and walked her toward their room. At least, it would be their room from this point forward.

22

Once in their room, Mia took his hand in hers and pressed her body against his. She loved the feel of his firm muscles as he moved his arms and body. When she pressed herself against him tightly, she could feel their movement against her breasts and she loved that it made her nipples hard.

His arms wrapped around her waist pulling her closer to him as she wrapped her arms around his shoulders and her legs around his waist.

"I'm hard as a fucking rock right now."

She giggled lightly in his ear. "I know."

His hands slid to cup the cheeks of her ass and his fingers moved further underneath and stroked her opening. Even with layers of fabric between his fingers and her body, the moisture surged between her legs. Huffing out a long breath, she sucked his earlobe and nipped it lightly before swirling her tongue around the shell of his ear.

"Jesus." He husked.

He moved efficiently and rather gracefully as he closed the door between this room and Creed's room while she still clung to him. Then he whisked them to the bathroom, reached in and turned the shower on to warm. His lips sought hers and his tongue plunged between her lips and swirled all around her mouth. Their tongues danced together, twisting and tasting while their lips moved together.

Caiden set her gently on top of the counter in the bathroom; his fingers eagerly removed her blouse and her bra within a matter of seconds. He bent and sucked on her left breast while his right hand squeezed and massaged the other. All too soon he switched and groaned; She felt the vibration all the way down to her toes. Her hands pushed into his hair and held his head tightly to her.

He straightened and pulled his t-shirt overhead, letting it fall on top of her clothes. His pants followed, then his briefs, and he stood before her gloriously naked, his toned muscles perfectly defined, his cock rigid and ready. Caiden wasted no time, tugging at her slacks, then sliding her forward off the counter and pushing her slacks and panties down over her hips.

He lifted her to the counter once again and pulled her to the edge, the tip of his cock at her entrance.

"Watch me disappear into you Mia," he commanded gruffly.

She watched in wonder and delight as his cock slid into her body and pulled back out, glistening with her juices. He pushed back in again and her breathing hitched. It felt different like this. She wasn't closing her eyes and feeling it, she was watching it and experiencing a whole new level of want. His breathing grew shallow and she realized hers had as well.

Her legs rested against his back just enough to relax them a bit, but Caiden held them higher as he continued to pump into her. She rested her hands behind her on the counter, but she couldn't look away as their bodies slickened with sweat while working to achieve their respective orgasms.

Caiden let go of her left leg and slid his fingers up and around her clit which caused her to spasm as he hit the perfect spot. He smiled slightly once he found it and continued to manipulate her clit until she cried out his name. Immediately he grabbed her leg again and increased his speed pumping into her body until he groaned and his orgasm shot through him. The muscles in his neck strained and his hands pulled her tightly to him.

Once he'd recovered slightly, he pulled her forward, his softening cock still inside of her and carried her to the shower. Once inside, he let her slide down his body, but she held on to his arms tightly because her knees shook and she was afraid she'd fall.

He smiled down at her. "I've got you."

He wrapped his arms around her and they stood for several minutes as the warm water splashed on them. As soon as she felt she could stand on her own, she relaxed her hold on him and stepped back slightly. "Wow."

"Yeah. Wow."

He squirted shampoo in her hair and washed it. His fingers massaging her scalp, then her neck then back up to her scalp again. He reached for the bar of soap as she rinsed the shampoo away and he began rubbing it all over her body, starting with her breasts, then over her belly and down to her sensitive clit. He played with her body like a toy, gently touching, cleaning, and admiring every inch of her. She couldn't remember anything she'd enjoyed more: other than the orgasm she'd just had.

She took the soap from his hands and repeated what he'd just done to her on his body. The slickness of the soapy water as her hands roamed over the muscles and planes of his body was sexy. But when she slid her hands down to wrap around his cock, and found it once again rigid, she had to rethink what she enjoyed more. She pumped his cock, base to tip over and over, watching as the pre-cum formed at the tip. Sliding her hands down to his balls, she found them firm and tight. She enlarged her movements to include his balls, every time she swept down to the base of his cock. Her fingers swept around his balls and she enjoyed when they tightened further.

Mia moved the bar of soap around his waist while holding his rigid cock in her left hand, her thumb rolling over the tip, and she slid the bar of soap between the cheeks of his ass and swirled her forefinger over the puckered hole. He groaned and she ventured to push her finger into him, the tightness making it difficult but not impossible to penetrate him. Once she had her finger in to the first knuckle she felt his cock pulse, so she pushed in further. His hands stilled on her body and his breathing became choppy. She pulled her finger out and pushed back in further and felt his cock pulse again. One more time and he came on her hand, his grunts of pleasure loud next to her ear.

"Is that a first time for you Caiden?"

"Yes."

"Good."

23

Caiden slipped his boots on and tied them. He stood away from the side of the bed and turned to watch Mia sleep. She was beautiful every day but in sleep, relaxed and warm and peaceful, she emitted an angelic aura. Her long dark hair, fanned out over the white pillowcase, made an enticing picture. He had his hands in her hair last night, washing it, then later, running the silky strands through his fingers as she slept. It was like living the dreams he'd had in the past of how it would be if she were alive. Now he needed to work to make sure she had a clear name and didn't have to worry about Dominick Fucking Nelson coming after her. They'd put that son of a bitch away for what he'd done, not only to Mia but to countless others.

Inhaling deeply, he quietly opened the door to Creed's room and stepped inside. Creed was working on his laptop when he entered and barely glanced up at him.

"Did anyone come for the phones?"

Creed shook his head. "No. They likely were onto what we were doing and they didn't bother. But, Deacon has reversed the tracking and we're just now able to track them. I'm waiting for the connection to lock into place then we'll find those bastards."

Caiden sat at the foot of the bed directly behind Creed so he could watch the computer screen. The little spinning wheel was still moving in a holding pattern.

"Deacon also sent you the link on your computer; you'll need to make the connection too."

"Okay." Caiden opened his laptop and logged on. He saw the email from Deacon and clicked it to see what he had to say about the reverse tracking.

To: Caiden Marx

From: Deacon Smythe

Date: March 18 4:38 a.m.

Caid,

I've set up the tracking so it now tracks whoever was watching the women. It's not that sophisticated of a system and was fairly easy, but I did have to get through a firewall to complete the setup.

I've been able to locate three separate systems accessing the tracking and it may not take them long to figure out that they're the ones being tracked now. Since they've likely figured out that someone on our end has removed the tracing from the girls, they'll be wary. Click the link below to set this up on your laptop.

Later - Deac.

Caiden clicked the link in the email and watched his computer connect to the tracking system. Within a couple of minutes, he was set and ready to see what was happening. He noted the system tracked by using green dots for the locations of the phones they were tracking, and though the phone numbers populated on the screen, they didn't know who belonged with what number. He noted that one of the phones was moving; the other two were stationary at the moment.

Enlarging the map of the city to see where the moving phone was going, he saw that it was downtown. He enlarged the map again and checked the streets around it. He blew the map up larger and read all the street names in that area. His heart raced and the hairs on the back of his neck stood up. Mia lived on that street. One of them was hanging out close to Mia's apartment.

"Creed, the one on Broad Street?"

Creed looked at his computer and enlarged the maps to see the street names. "Yeah."

"That's where Mia lives. Same block."

The little green dot stopped moving and Caiden watched it to see if it was hanging out or going into the building. It stayed in one place.

Caiden picked up his phone and called Piper.

"Morning."

"Morning Pipes. One of the assholes tracking the women is now standing outside Mia's apartment building."

"You're sure?"

"Yes. Get your wig and meet me in the underground parking garage at the building. I'll text you the address."

His fingers flew over the screen, typing in the address before he sent the text.

As soon as she saw it she replied, "I'll be there in twelve minutes."

Caiden chuckled. "Exactly twelve?"

"Well GPS says twelve and I'm ready to go, so yeah, twelve."

"Roger. Put on your comm unit Pipes."

Caiden chuckled and watched the tracking lights to make sure none of them moved. As soon as one did, he'd be watching.

"I'm off to meet Pipes at Mia's place. We'll capture at least one of these assholes today. If we have to do it one at a time, that's just the way it is. When Mia wakes, let her know I'll be back as soon as I can."

"Roger that."

Caid closed his laptop and dropped it in its carry case, then quietly opened the door to see Mia still sleeping. He closed it and looked at Creed. "Call me if that phone moves."

"Will do bro."

Caiden left the hotel room and power walked to the elevator, then double-timed it to the garage area. Climbing into the SUV, he started it up and pulled out of the parking spot without hesitating. He was on the street navigating early morning Vegas traffic faster than he anticipated and happily the wait time was a lot less than he'd imagined it could be.

His phone rang and he answered without looking at the screen.

"Marx."

"Roman here."

"It's going to take some getting used to hearing your new name."

Piper chuckled. "It's taking some time getting used to saying it."

Caiden laughed. "I bet. What's up?"

"I'm behind the building but can't get into the garage, I don't have keys."

"Is there a place to park back there on the street?"

"Yes."

"Perfect, park there. I'll be back there in a couple of minutes."

"Ten-four."

Caiden navigated a few more corners and streets and finally found himself pulling in behind Piper.

He attached his comm unit and got out of his SUV after checking the area. "Anyone move?"

Creed responded, "No."

"Okay, both Piper and I are here now, keep track of it."

24

Mia stretched and looked around for Caiden. Sitting up, she noticed that his clothes were gone and so were his boots. A slight frown formed on her lips and she flopped back down on the bed. Her thoughts drifted to last night and their love-making and she flipped her frown around.

Then she remembered the women and wondered if they'd captured the traffickers last night. She got up and dressed quickly, grimacing as she realized she needed to pick up some clean clothes. Caiden was going to need to let her go back to her place today and pack some clothes and that was that.

She used the bathroom and brushed her teeth with her finger and rinsed several times with water. And she needed a toothbrush and a hairbrush and her makeup. Good gravy she was ill prepared for being here at all.

She padded across the room to the adjoining door and knocked on it. Creed responded, "Come on in Mia."

She opened the door and stepped into the room, quickly assessing that Caiden wasn't there.

"Where did he go?"

"Actually he went to your apartment building. He's meeting Piper there." Creed pointed to his computer.

She stepped up to see his screen and Creed indicated green dots. "These are the phones of the men we're tracking. This one..." he pointed to one of them, "is near your apartment building." Creed enlarged the map so she could see the location clearly. Her stomach twisted and threatened to lose its meager contents. She sat weak-kneed at the foot of the bed behind Creed and he moved over just a bit so she could see clearly.

"We don't know who it is, since there are three of them to watch, but Piper is going into the building wearing her dark wig so whoever is watching will think it's you. She'll be ready and as soon as the dot starts moving I'll let them know." He held up his comm unit microphone.

Creed plugged one end of the comm unit into his computer. "You'll be able to hear them now."

Caiden's voice came through. "Okay, Piper is entering the building at the front."

"Roger."

Piper then responded, "I'm in the lobby. I'm first going to walk to the bank of mailboxes, then I'll stand at the elevator. What floor is Mia on?"

"Third floor." Caiden answered.

"Roger."

There was silence for a few minutes then the green dot outside the building began moving toward the door.

"The phone is on the move toward the building Pipes."

"Roger. I'm now walking to the elevator."

"They're crossing the street."

"Roger."

"The target is now walking into the building."

"Roger. I'm just stepping onto the elevator. I see a man entering the building. I'm closing the doors."

A moment of silence then Piper said, "He saw me and started walking quickly to the elevator, but I got the doors closed first. I'll wait just around the corner from the elevator when I get off."

Caiden then responded. "Pipes give me some description, I'm coming into the building now."

"Fatigues. Army boots. Green sweatshirt. Not Dildo."

Creed sat back a bit frustrated that it wasn't Dildo.

Mia lay her hand on her stomach. If it had had any food in it, it wouldn't have stayed down, and her empty belly twisted and twirled as she listened to Caiden and Piper. Someone dangerous was in the building with them. They could get shot. She took a deep breath and let it out slowly in hopes it would help her relax. Creed looked over at her briefly and grinned.

"It's okay, they're very good at their jobs."

"Is Mia with you Creed?"

"Yes and she seems a bit unnerved."

"It's okay, Baby, this'll be over soon. I'm inside." He was quiet for a moment. "Pipes, Army wannabe is in the elevator. I'm taking the stairs."

"Roger. I'm in the middle of the hall in the janitor's closet. Door's open and I'm just inside."

Mia could hear Caiden's labored breathing and she worried for him. She swallowed, trying to wet her throat and her eyes locked on the moving green dot. She wanted to say something but clapped her hand over her mouth instead.

"Pipes, he's out of the elevator."

The creak of a squeaky door could be heard, and Caiden's labored breathing. Then nothing. Mia tried imagining where he was on her floor. She was on the farthest end of the hall from the stairs, another safety issue for her. She debated being close in case she had to make an escape but worried it would be a way for Dominick to get in undetected because the stairwell was hidden from the lobby.

Caiden's voice sounded stern, "She's not home."

"Fuck you, asshole."

Caiden laughed. "You think you're going to just grab her and traffic her like the others?"

Mia listened, wide-eyed, both hands now holding her mouth shut.

"You don't know what you're talking about."

"I believe I do."

She heard rustling, maybe a tussle, then Caid's voice.

"Don't do it."

Bang. Bang. Bang.

Then silence.

"Creed, call 911."

Mia's eyes glistened with tears and just as quickly they streamed down her cheeks. Creed responded, "How many are down?"

Piper responded, "Just one. The perp. We're fine."

A sob broke from Mia's throat and she ran to her room then her bathroom to compose herself while Creed called police. Mia splashed water on her face then pulled a towel off the rack and dried it. She leaned against the counter where last night she'd been with Caiden and she wondered how he did this kind of work. Could she tolerate knowing he was in danger most of the time while working? How did other wives or girlfriends do it? And Piper's husband, Royce? Did he hate this? For that matter, were there other wives? There was so much she didn't know, and Caiden had promised her a long chat, which they had neglected to have last night. But today, it was definitely going to happen.

25

Caiden walked into the hotel room four hours after he shot Tannon Marcel. They didn't have all the information they needed on Marcel. Most notably, who did he work for? But, he'd called Emmy and she was taking care of speaking with their police chief to share information.

Creed was doing pushups on the floor and Mia wasn't in the room.

"How many is that, like three?"

"Fuck off, Caid."

Caiden laughed and walked into the adjoining room to see Mia lying on the bed studying her notes.

"Hey."

A sob escaped her throat as she launched herself off the bed and ran to him. He scooped her up and hugged her tightly.

"Oh my God, I'm so happy to see you. You're not hurt? Did you get hurt? Is Piper alright?"

He chuckled and set her feet on the ground.

"So you were worried about me?"

She slapped at his arms. "That's not funny."

"I think it is."

"You don't have a very good sense of humor then."

"Ouch."

"Caiden!"

"Okay. Yes, I'm fine. Yes, Piper's fine. No, neither of us was hurt."

"What about the man in the building?"

"Well, he was hurt. But not fatally."

"How do you joke about that stuff?"

Caiden took a deep breath and let it out. He took her hand and led her to the bed then sat facing her.

"Baby, this is our job. We're passionate about what we do, and we do it for women like you, and children who otherwise don't have anyone looking out for them."

"It's just..." She looked out the window a minute then huffed out a breath. "It's just that it was really scary listening to that and not knowing."

He nodded and smiled at her. "Maybe you won't want to listen next time or any time. It goes like that. Not always but it does. We have communication with each other and we have teammates that will do anything it takes to make sure we all get out alive."

Mia nodded but said nothing.

"These people we help, baby, they need us."

"They do. I know that for a fact. I've heard all the women you rescued at Container World say it over and over how grateful they are that you saved them. They'd felt hopeless and scared and desperate. Then you all broke in and saved them. They think you're all gods or something."

"God has a nice ring to it."

Mia socked him pretty hard in the arm. "Ouch."

"I'm serious Caiden. Are there other team members that are married? How do they handle it all?"

Caiden leaned forward and took both of her hands in his. "I'll tell you what. When we're finished here, we're going to West Virginia to clear your name and make sure Dominick Fucking Nelson goes down for all he's done. Then, I'll take you to Indiana where our headquarters is, and you can meet the other wives and husbands."

"Husbands?"

"Yes, well, we're connected to another group called GHOST. Our respective compounds are next door to each other and connected via an underground tunnel. There are nine GHOST members, all of them married to smart, gorgeous women and two of the GHOST members are married to each other—Jax and Dodge, and Gaige is married to Sophie who also pitches in when needed. Then in RAPTOR we have nine team members, three female operatives; Charly, Piper, and Emmy, and six male operatives; Diego, Donovan, Creed, Falcon, whose father is in GHOST, Deacon, and myself. Diego, Donovan, Charly, and Piper are married. You'll hear all their stories and they'll tell you how they deal with all the scary stuff that happens. Plus, many of them now have children so there are little ones running around the compounds too."

"Wow, that's a bit...overwhelming."

"I'm sure it sounds that way now, but once you meet everyone, you'll see they're just people like us. One of the women, Isabella, is a doctor, one, Roxanne, is a lawyer. Hadleigh is a social worker, Shelby is a childcare provider, Charly's husband Sam is a cop. It's how they met actually."

"Okay. I'll look forward to meeting them."

He squeezed her hands. "I'm going to set up a video chat with Roxanne, Hawk's wife. She's an attorney. I want you there to explain what happened to you and your mom. We'll need Roxanne's help in slogging through the legal workings of your situation. We'll want her to work with police to ensure that if you come forward and give testimony as to what happened to your mom, that they won't press charges against you for delivering illegal substances and leaving the scene of a crime. There might be other charges and Roxanne will work all that out before we say anything. But you were a minor, so I would be suspicious of anyone wanting to press charges."

Mia leaned forward and sucked in a few deep breaths. "Oh my god, I hadn't even thought of charges against me. I didn't know that could happen from so long ago."

"I'd guess the statute of limitations is up, but we'll want to make sure before we go waltzing into the police station. Roxanne will help us with all of that."

"Okay."

"Hey, Caiden." Creed said from the adjoining room. "It looks like one of our phones got on a plane and is heading to Miami. Apparently word is out about Marcel. The other phone just went dead, so I'm sure whoever is heading to Miami will kill their phone soon as well."

"Fuck. You think it's Dildo?"

"No way to know man. But, Donovan has the phone number in case he gets the same number on a new phone. We'll try that after we give him enough time to land and get a new phone. The other one, well, we'll have to keep watching that one too and see if they stick around or fly the coop."

Mia looked up, "Can you check and see if Nadia Petrov is on a plane to Miami?"

"I'll check that out right now."

Caiden leaned in and touched his forehead to hers. "You sure you don't want to be an operative?"

26

Mia sat at the desk in her hotel room writing down the pertinent information of what had happened to her and her mother. Caiden had asked her to write it down so she didn't forget anything. She'd mused about writing a book about it one day; she still might. This could be the beginnings of it if she got brave enough to do it.

She stared out the window in between the horrible details. They still brought her to tears and she could still see her mother's eyes staring at her and the red streak across her neck just before she mouthed, "Run."

She jumped up out of her chair and walked to the bathroom and splashed more water on her face. Caiden and Creed were in the other room talking to their boss, Emmy, about what had happened, she heard other voices on the conference call too, some of the operatives Caiden had mentioned earlier. From what she'd heard, they were trying to plan out what to do from here. A team might go to Miami to see if they could track whomever left here. And Emmy sure did hate Dildo. They all did, but she had a harder time masking her hatred when she said his name. Mia liked Emmy already.

She dried her face again and left the bathroom to finish writing down the details of her fucked-up life. She'd been writing for more than two hours and her fingers were sore, so she decided to type it into her computer.

"Hey, are you getting hungry?"

She smiled at Caiden, who poked his head around the door. She could still hear the meeting going on behind him.

"Yeah."

"I hate to ask, but would you call room service and ask for food to be brought up here? They'll put it on our room tab. Order what you want, but Creed and I are starving so order a lot of it."

She giggled when he winked at her, and she had that silly high-school feeling in her belly that she'd had all those years ago when he looked at her.

"Okay. I'll get you something delicious."

"Thank you, baby. Gotta go."

He disappeared back in their room and she looked up the room service number and called down. She'd decided on wings and ordered four dozen of them with fries, and a large side of celery sticks. Then she ordered beers for them all, two each—today was a beer drinking day for sure. She hoped they could drink; they were still sort of on the job.

Setting the phone back in its cradle, she opened her computer and continued writing out the details of her ordeal. And as she wrote, she tried not thinking about the fact that she could go to jail. Caiden said Roxanne would help her and they would first compile a file on Dominick to offer to police as a bargaining tool. It seemed likely that police would prefer to get a piece of shit like Dominick off the streets versus sending Mia to jail for something she did as a minor, but weirder things have happened.

A knock on the door startled her out of her writing and she froze. Swallowing, she slowly made her way to the door, standing on her toes to look through the peephole. Force of habit.

She stepped back as Caiden entered the room and watched over her, which thrilled her because of his protection. Once again, he made her feel safe.

"I have four dozen wings, fries, and beer for this room."

"Yes, thank you. Please set it all on the table."

She looked at Caiden and he mouthed, "Four dozen?"

She giggled and nodded and Caiden rubbed his belly.

He turned to Creed. "Wings and beer!"

"Now you're talking." Creed responded.

The waiter turned to her with the bill, but Caiden took it and signed his name then handed it back. "Thank you."

The waiter looked at the bill; his eyes rounded when he saw the tip that was left, then his smile grew ear to ear. "Thank you so much sir. Enjoy your meal."

Mia began opening the containers of food and the aroma that filled the room was like a slice of heaven. Her stomach growled and she realized she was quite hungry, too.

Caiden kissed her lips lightly then said, "Dig in. Once Creed grazes the table there won't be much left."

Creed laughed but shot Caiden the finger and Mia felt light and happy once again. She'd missed having close friends over the years. She had friends and people who certainly stepped up to help her, but she didn't have a close friend or friends. She didn't have that BFF that was so tossed about on social media. She couldn't afford it. But sitting here with Caiden and Creed, she could feel their friendship and the bond they had, and she imagined she had a little bit of that too.

"Mia, baby, this is delicious and so needed. I thought I was going to eat my computer about ten minutes ago I was so fucking hungry."

Creed had a mouthful of hot chicken and said, "Christ, me too. We've got to start eating better. I'm fucking sick of meal bars."

She giggled and took a bite of her chicken and had to agree, this beat meal bars all to hell and back.

Caiden pulled three beers from the Styrofoam cooler they were brought in and opened one and handed it to her then set one on the table in front of Creed, taking the last one for himself.

"What, you aren't going to open mine too?"

"Fuck no, you can open your own damned beer."

Creed laughed and popped the top on the can of beer and took a good long swig. "My god that tastes good."

27

Caiden washed his hands in Mia's bathroom, their bathroom, and came back into the room. Mia and Creed were both relaxed and looked quite full and happy.

"Mia, during our conference call with headquarters a couple of decisions were made. Deacon, Falcon, and Diego are heading to Miami. Creed is staying here, and Piper will work with him to locate and apprehend the third person who we believe to still be here. You and I will fly out to West Virginia in the morning. Roxanne will meet us there and we'll go over everything with her."

Mia sat up straight, her eyes rounded and her lips parted slightly, but she said nothing.

He walked over to sit at the foot of the bed closest to where she sat and leaned his elbows on his knees. "I thought you wanted to do that. Clear your name and bring Nelson down."

He watched her throat as she swallowed, then she turned to look at him. "I do. It's just that..." She inhaled and let it out slowly. "It's just that it now feels real."

Creed looked over at her, a smile on his face. "It's real Mia. And it's scary. Remember those women we saved and how scared they were? It's scary like that. But Caiden will be with you, and behind the scenes we're all working on a file on Dominick. You'll have plenty of ammo to use against him and you'll have a giant bargaining tip to use with the police."

"Behind the scenes?"

Caiden felt sorry for her. "Honey, my friends at RAPTOR know you mean a lot to me and they are willing to step up and help you out. You have a huge team of people behind you. Pulling for you. Willing to assist in any way we can."

A tear slid silently down her cheek and he watched it. Then he leaned forward and swiped it with his thumb.

"I've never had..." She cleared her throat. "I'm overwhelmed, actually."

Creed clapped his hands together. "You've got this. I'll expect to hear all about it the second it comes together."

"If it comes together," she whispered.

Caiden reached forward and took her hand. "Mia, baby, it will come together."

She inhaled deeply again and let it out in a huff. "Okay. I'm pulling up my big girl panties and facing this head on. I'm sick of running and I'm sick of hiding. I didn't do anything wrong. Not intentionally anyway."

He smiled at her. "There you go, and I'll be there every step of the way."

"Thank you." She stared deeply into his eyes and his heart, wow, it felt like she could fly.

"You're welcome."

Mia turned to Creed. "Thank you, too. I don't have anything to offer you in return except my gratitude."

Creed smiled at her and nodded. "Your gratitude is more than enough, Mia. Just keep my friend here happy and it's all good."

Mia's head cocked to the left, then turned to look at him. She smiled, broader this time. "I'll do my best."

Caiden winked at her because honestly, his throat was constricted, and he wasn't sure he could say anything without sounding like a blubbering baby. He heaved out a breath. "Okay Mia, let's get rolling. We have to go to your apartment and pack up some things to take with us."

"Is it safe?"

Caiden shrugged. "I'll be honest and tell you we don't know. But Creed is coming with us, and Piper is on standby if we need her, so I think you'll be as safe as you can be. But, nothing is one hundred percent. That's the honest-to-goodness down and dirty. But, since they know we're on to them, I find it doubtful they'll be there again so soon after this afternoon. Anything is possible, though. So, we'll take precautions and be vigilant."

"Okay."

Mia stood and began cleaning up the food containers and he and Creed pitched in to help. Then they got ready to go.

He and Creed went into the other room and strapped on weapons and comm units while Mia put her shoes on.

"Here, wear this comm unit, baby."

He helped her slide the wire up the back of her shirt and attached the box to her waistband. "This is just in case we get separated. You'll be able to talk to Creed, Piper, and me at any time."

"Okay."

They walked to the elevator, he and Mia side by side and Creed following behind. As they neared the elevator, he pulled Mia behind him and in front of Creed, tapped the button on the wall and they waited in formation. He was grateful she didn't put up a fuss, she was going along with whatever. Just like he remembered from years gone by. She'd always been up for anything, within reason. She was a good girl, but she was eager to do any new activities or try her hand at hunting to be with him or learn about racing because he loved it. He tried returning the favor by watching chick flicks to please her, mostly because she'd rest against him and he could feel her soft skin or smell her hair.

The elevator opened and they quietly stepped in. He stood partially in front of her, Creed was on the other side of her.

They rode the elevator down quietly, and stepped off at the lobby, and walked through the casino and to the parking garage, Caiden held his breath as they walked. They hopped inside the SUV, Mia in the back, he and Creed in front.

As they worked their way toward her apartment complex Piper joined with her comm unit.

"I'm on, everyone. Mia, everything is going to be alright."

Mia responded softly. "Thank you, Piper. I appreciate all everyone is doing to help."

As they neared the apartment building, he directed Creed. "Take the back street and enter through the underground garage."

"Roger."

28

Mia's hands shook and her palms were sweaty. After what had just gone on here, she didn't want to be back. But she did want most of her things. She'd had to start over with only the clothes on her back once in her life. That was enough. She'd scrounged Goodwill stores and the donation bins at the Y when she'd first arrived here. As grateful as she was for those clothes, she had no desire to go back to that life.

Creed parked the SUV and Caiden turned to her. "Ready?"

She nodded, cleared her throat and finally managed to say, "Yeah."

He exited the SUV, opened her door and held his hand out to help her exit. Once she was out of the truck, he placed his hands on her shoulders, bent down so they were eye to eye and smiled at her. "We're going in and not staying long. Take absolutely what you think you can't live without. The rest can be replaced. Once we get everything straightened out in West Virginia, we can come back and deal with the rest, however you want to deal. Okay?"

"Yeah."

He kissed her lips briefly, then took her hand and led her from the parking area to the elevator. Every noise, every sound, every movement in the corner of her eye scared the bejeezus out of her.

The elevator was empty, which she was grateful for, and when it stopped on her floor she inhaled and prepared for...whatever was to happen.

They stepped out of the elevator, Caiden in front of her, Creed behind and walked with purpose to her door. Caiden stopped in front of her door and Mia pulled her keys from her purse. But her fingers shook, so he gently took them and opened her door. He went in first and held up his forefinger for her to wait. He disappeared inside and her heart thudded so strongly in her chest she thought she'd pass out. Perhaps she shouldn't have had that beer. But she was grateful for the one waiting for her back at the hotel.

She turned her head and saw the police tape across the stairwell door and saw the spot of blood on the floor and smeared on the wall where apparently Marcel had slid down the wall. It wasn't a large amount of blood, but enough that you could tell something bad happened there.

"Don't look at it, Mia," Creed coached her.

She faced forward and waited for Caiden to appear. Had he been in there an hour? It sure felt like it.

Finally he stepped in the doorway and nodded.

She walked in and it felt like a strange place to her. She'd barely thought about coming back here during the two days she'd been gone. She only wanted her clothing. She went first to her closet and pulled her suitcase out and lay it on the bed. Then she quickly pulled clothing from the closet.

"Mia, do you have another suitcase?"

"Yes." She bent and pulled it from the back of the closet and handed it to Caiden. He unzipped it while she continued pulling clothes she wanted with her from their hangers.

"I'll fold these and put them in the suitcase, you keep pulling clothes you want to bring. You'll have to refold them when we get to the hotel."

She smiled at him. "I'm not worried about that at all. I just want to get out of here safely."

She walked to her dresser and pulled open her top drawer and scooped up her undergarments. She walked to the suitcase and hesitated.

Caiden looked at her face, then the clothing in her hands and stepped back. Relief flooded through her that he didn't insist on packing her underwear. Not that it was special and certainly not because she didn't think he'd take care of it, but it was so personal.

She shook her head at her ridiculousness. There were more important things to worry over.

She stepped into her bathroom and pulled a large cosmetic bag she'd purchased to match her suitcase. It had been what felt like a decadent purchase at the time. She fancied herself to be able to travel one day like the hawt reporter she dreamed of being. Sought after for interviews and speaking engagements. She shook her head at the silly thoughts and started loading her makeup, shampoo, conditioner, shower soap, nail stuff, and more into her bag and carried it all back into the bedroom.

Caiden was folding the last of her garments into the suitcase and she stopped and looked around.

"Mia, are there some personal things you want to bring with you?"

She walked to her bedside table and pulled out the only drawer it had in it. There was a small photograph of Caiden in his football uniform his senior year. And a newspaper clipping of her mother with her obituary attached to it. Her fingers shook when she looked at them, but Caiden's strong arms wrapped around her from behind, his lips next to her ear whispered, "You kept a picture of me?"

"I downloaded it off the internet when I was able and kept it."

"It looks like it's been held a lot. The dents and frayed edges give you away."

She only nodded and tears spilled from her eyes.

She turned in his arms. "I never stopped loving you, Caid. Never."

He pulled her into his body and she listened to his heartbeat increase, his breathing quick and raspy. "I never stopped loving you either Mia. Never. Always and forever."

Her arms wrapped around his waist and she pulled him close, her tears wetting the front of his t-shirt. How could she have been so lucky amid so much sorrow?

She sniffed and regretfully stepped back. "I have to blow my nose."

He kissed the top of her head. "Go on, we can resume this once we're safe at the hotel."

29

Caiden held Mia's hand as they walked across the tarmac to the private plane waiting for them.

"You have a private plane?"

"RAPTOR does."

"Holy cow. I had no idea."

"It was necessary. Sometimes we have to fly out in a hurry. Waiting for a commercial flight was a detriment and booking private flights was getting expensive. RAPTOR is making great money now and Emmy felt it was a necessary expense. Plus, our pilot Therese, is badass."

"You have a female pilot!"

He chuckled and pulled her ahead of him to climb the stairs to the plane. Inside, Therese waited to greet them.

"Hello Miss Gregory. Mr. Marx. We're ready to take off once you're in your seats."

"Thank you, Therese. Just give us about five minutes to settle in."

"Yes sir."

Therese stepped into the cockpit and Mia walked toward the seats in the plane.

"Wow, this is fabulous."

"It is. And Emmy had the plane fitted for us. We've got some big guys working with us, so we have some legroom."

"Amazing."

He chuckled as Mia looked around. Taking her suitcase, he tucked it in the luggage compartment along with his, wrapped the strap around the suitcases and closed the door. He found Mia sitting next to the window looking out on the tarmac and took the seat next to her.

"Buckle your seatbelt, Mia."

She turned to him then her brows furrowed slightly. She looked down in the seat and pulled the seatbelt up, clicking it into place.

"I've never flown before."

"You've never flown?"

She shook her head. "It wasn't safe. I couldn't."

"How did you get to assignments?"

"I usually managed to drive. If it was very far away, I'd do them remotely over a face-to-face chat session."

"And your editor allowed this?"

She shrugged. "I told him I was deathly afraid of flying, which I was, but not because of the flying part. It was because I never knew if someone was watching me."

He leaned forward and kissed her temple. "Baby, I'm so sorry for all you've been through."

A wistful smile graced her face, but she said nothing and he let it go at that. He took her right hand in his left and locked their fingers.

"When we begin to take off, you'll feel like you're being pushed into the seat for a few minutes until we get in the air. Then there will be times when you'll feel like we're going to drop from the sky. We won't, but be prepared. Sometimes the plane will shake as we go through turbulence. Therese will let us know what it is over the intercom. Otherwise, this is a great time to close your eyes and try to rest, we'll be in the air for around five hours. Maybe less."

"Okay."

Therese's voice was heard over the speaker system. "We're cleared for takeoff."

"Here we go, baby."

Her fingers squeezed his a bit tighter, and he smiled. Mia watched out the window the whole time and as the plane left the ground her excitement was palpable.

"Wow, we're flying."

He chuckled. "We sure are."

"This is fantastic. I always hoped I'd be able to fly."

"We'll fly as much as you want to."

"Really? Oh I don't even know where I'd want to go first."

She leaned over the arm of the seat and kissed his cheek. "Thank you, Caid."

He laughed then and kissed her lips. "We could join the mile-high club."

"What's that?"

"It's where you have sex once you're up above the clouds."

"Won't someone know?"

"We're the only ones here. Therese is flying the plane."

"She can't see back here?"

He laughed again. "No."

Mia's cheeks turned beet red, but her eyes were filled with excitement. She leaned in as if they had a big secret. "When can we do it?"

"As soon as Therese turns off the 'Fasten Seat belt light.'" He pointed above them to the light and Mia's eyes barely left it.

He pulled away a bit and lifted the chair arm between them and her smile grew. A chime sounded and he looked up to see the sign had gone off. Mia pulled her seat belt buckle open and turned to him. "Your seat or mine?"

"Mine." He unbuckled his seat belt and unsnapped his jeans. Then he unzipped them and shimmied them down to his knees.

He looked over at Mia only to see her fall to her knees before him; her warm wet mouth instantly slid over his rigid cock and he pushed his head back into the seat and closed his eyes.

"Oh God Mia, that feels fantastic."

Her tongue swirled around the tip of his cock before she sucked him into her mouth, adding pressure as she sucked. He groaned again and pushed his hips up into her mouth, his hands in her hair. "Mia." His breathing grew raspy and choppy, his balls pulled up painfully and just before his orgasm was about to explode, she pulled up and looked at him. She licked her lips and the sly smile that played on her face told him she wasn't done yet.

She stood and pulled her jeans off her hips and down her legs, then shimmied her panties down and stepped out of them. She straddled him, took his cock in her hand and placed him at her entrance then, while her eyes were locked on his, she slowly lowered herself onto him.

It was fucking amazing.

She rode him slow and steady for a while, then she increased her speed and rode him hard. They both grew warm, their skin slick with sweat their breathing rapid and heavy.

"Tell me when you're ready Caid."

"Fuck."

"Is that ready?"

"Fuck yes." He groaned.

She moved her hips back and forth, then up and down then back and forth and her climax was close. He held onto her hips enjoying the feel of their movement, her soft skin under his hands and when she groaned and pushed herself firmly onto him, he pushed his hips up into her and let his own release go.

"Fucking amazing."

30

Mia took a deep breath as they drove in the rental car to the hotel Caiden had secured. He opened her door and held his hand out to help her down.

"It's going to be fine Mia. I won't let anything happen to you. If Roxanne can't secure your freedom, we'll go right back."

"I know." She huffed out a breath and chanted to herself to relax. Everything Caiden had done to this point had been spot on.

He held her hand as they walked into the lobby of the hotel. He showed his driver's license and the clerk checked them in. They were on the third floor and had a view of the pool, according to the clerk who seemed to look at Caiden a little longer than she should have. But Caiden didn't seem to notice, which made her heart happy. The pretty hotel clerk likely came with a ton less baggage than she did.

Caiden handed her their room keys and he pulled both suitcases along as they strode to the elevator. They stepped in with another couple who'd clearly just left the pool area as they stood dripping on the floor in the elevator. They were giggling and making eyes at each other and Mia and Caiden stared straight ahead just wanting this to be over.

As soon as the doors opened, he waited for her to go before him, then he pulled their suitcases along the hall to their room. Once inside, she looked around the room and was pleasantly surprised at the decor and the cleanliness of the room. She walked to the window and saw the children in brightly-colored bathing suits splashing, playing, yelling, and laughing and she couldn't help but smile.

Caiden stepped to the window alongside her and grinned. "Cute."

"They are."

He never turned to look at her, he just stared out the window. "Do you want them?"

Her brows furrowed and she looked up at him. "I'm sorry?"

He stared into her eyes, his were serious. "Do you want kids?"

She cocked her head to the right and stared into his gorgeous blue eyes. She smiled, "I'd never let myself think about it before. I didn't think I could keep myself and a baby safe. I didn't want a baby to have to live like I did." She looked out the window again, then into Caiden's eyes. "I'd want them with you. No one else. You."

He swallowed and turned to her. "My job is unpredictable, and you know it's dangerous. There will be times I won't be around sometimes for a few days at a time. You'd be alone with the baby or babies, but you'd be safe. You need to think about that."

She nodded. "I'll keep it in mind."

His lips pressed softly against hers, then he wrapped his arms around her and held her close.

His phone rang and he sighed before stepping back and pulling it from his pocket.

"Marx...Oh, of course. We just checked in. Your room or ours? Roger."

He pocketed his phone and smiled. "Roxanne is here. We're to go up to her room and chat."

Mia looked down at her clothing, "Do I need to change or something?"

He chuckled, "You're beautiful just as you are."

She nodded and the butterflies in her stomach made her nauseous. She lay a hand on her tummy. Caiden walked to the door and waited for her to be ready, then he opened it and they walked out together, hand in hand.

"She's just above us."

Mia nodded. He'd said she was smart. Beautiful and efficient. She wasn't sure what she was more intimidated by, the smarts or the beauty. They exited the elevator and Caiden led them to Roxanne's door and knocked.

Mia was not ready for the woman who answered the door. Stunning, with long white hair that hung to her small waist. Long legs encased in denim, a perfect smile, and a warm hug for Caiden.

"Caiden. It's so good to see you again. Come in."

Roxanne stood back, and they entered her room, which looked like their room.

"Roxanne, this is Mia. Mia, Roxanne."

Roxanne pulled her into a hug and held her close. "You don't worry, we're going to get this sorted in no time."

"Thank you so much."

She smelled fantastic. She looked amazing and when she led them to the table in her room, and the spare bed, lined neatly with papers, Mia was blown away.

"Let me show you what I've been up to. Actually RAPTOR and GHOST have all had something to do with this. We even had Jared Timms do some questionable snooping for us. Nothing we could ever use in court, but knowledge is power, and the police will want this knowledge, believe me."

"Who's Jared Timms?" She questioned.

"Ah, well..." Roxanne laughed. "Jared is a special individual who has the uncanniest ways of sneaking into other people's computers and servers."

Mia's eyes grew round and she watched Roxanne glance quickly at Caiden then back to her. Caiden chuckled. "Baby, in our line of work, we sometimes have to work outside the lines of the law. It's a means to an end. We make sure the information we gather can be corroborated with legally obtained facts, but sometimes we need a leg up as to where to begin looking. Jared doesn't work for us, he's more or less a hired gun. He likes it that way and so do we."

"Okay."

Roxanne nodded, "So, what we've found is here." She walked to a stack of papers on the far side of the bed near the pillows. "Dominick Nelson is a piece of shit. He's been trafficking drugs for years. He changes out his couriers so often police don't know who's running for him day by day. That's by design. Jared was able to go back as far as twenty years. We looked at the girls in high school twenty years ago and matched them up with profiles. Good girls. Cheerleaders. School leaders such as student council, 4-H, Girl Scouts, etc. He seemed to focus on those girls because police wouldn't suspect them at all. Then we took those girls and looked at who suddenly had grade drop-offs. Stopped socializing. Some dropped out of school. Three from this oldest class alone ran away. More on that in a minute. Then we did the class from nineteen years ago and ran the same profiles. Then eighteen, seventeen, on and on. We crossed those who showed a decline in grades, dropped out or generally changed and tried linking them with Nelson. Either through security cameras, jobs, and the like."

Mia shook her head. "Jobs?"

"Ah yes, this is where Nelson tried to look legit. He started two businesses in Smoky Ridge to look credible. He had an ice cream shop, the Double Dipping. I'm assuming pun intended. And he had a laundromat/dry cleaner's named Dirty Duds. Also a pun."

"I remember those. Do you Caid?"

"I do. Never would have dreamed he had anything to do with them."

"Yes, he wanted it that way I'm sure. But what he also did was meet some of his employees this way. So we crossed the lists of the good girls with anyone who worked in one of Nelson's businesses and traced what happened to them. We've found more than forty-one who were in some way connected with Nelson who also ended up jumping off the path they were on. Some of them are in jail. Some are dispersed. We didn't try to track anyone down, but we compiled a list that we're happy to offer to police for them to investigate in exchange for your freedom. As well as your promise to testify that you witnessed Nelson kill your mother."

Roxanne stopped and turned to her. "I'm so very sorry for your loss Mia. I can't even imagine. If it makes any difference at all, both of my parents were murdered a few years ago. I do understand a little."

Mia's bottom lip quivered. "Thank you. I'm sorry for your loss as well."

Roxanne's soft smile reassured her, and Mia began to feel less intimidated, though Roxanne was a presence to be certain.

"Caiden tells me you're married."

Roxanne's gorgeous smile widened joyfully. She pulled her phone up and turned it around to show her a picture of one super huge but sexy man with bulging muscles and a big smile holding a small child of about two years old."

"This is Hawk. He's a presence for certain, and that little guy is Hank Jr."

"Oh my, he's adorable."

"He's the spitting image of his dad and he eats just about as much, too."

They all laughed and Mia looked into her light-blue eyes. "How do you handle Hawk being away? How do you handle the fear when he's gone?"

Roxanne looked at her and smiled softly. "He is very good at his job. They all are. What he does is part of who he is. He loves it. So, I had to learn to set my fear aside and trust that what will be will be. I know that sounds trite and I don't mean it to be. But, we have a strong group of sister wives, so to speak, and we're all in the same boat. We share worries, sorrows, childcare, schooling and the like. We're fortunate that our daily needs are met by excellent house staff and we enjoy being together. So, it really is just trusting that he knows what he's doing."

31

He listened as Mia readied herself in the bathroom. Today Roxanne had an appointment set up with them at the police station. Mia had been restless last night, which meant they didn't get a lot of sleep, but Roxanne felt confident that things would work out and he believed her. He had to believe her. He'd finally gotten Mia back after years of believing she was dead.

Mia walked into the room. The dark circles under her eyes a testament to the night she'd had, but she was still so beautiful and precious.

"Do you want to eat something light before we go?"

She lay her hand across her stomach and shook her head. "I'm afraid it wouldn't stay down."

"I'll bring something with us and afterwards if you need something, I'll have it ready."

She walked to him and wrapped her arms around his waist. "I don't know how I got along all these years without you. No matter what happens today, please know that I love you and I'm so very grateful for all you've done for me."

He grabbed her shoulders and pulled her back slightly so he could look into her eyes. "No. You need to believe this is all going to be fine, Mia."

"But I did wrong. I did deliver the drugs."

"But you didn't know it was drugs."

"The police may not care about that."

He laid his forefinger under her chin. "They want Nelson, not some girl who sixteen years ago was manipulated by Nelson. You saw all that Roxanne had on him. The police will want that."

She looked into his eyes for a long time, then she nodded. "That's true."

His phone rang and he pulled it from his pocket. "It's Roxanne."

He tapped the answer icon. "Good morning. Are you ready to go?"

"Yes, I'll meet you in the lobby."

"We're on our way down."

Without another word, he took Mia's hand and walked to the door and sent up a silent prayer that today would be a good day for them. Then he planned on taking her to his parents' house and explaining everything that had happened.

They climbed into Caiden's rental car; Mia opted to sit in the back seat. He watched her in the mirror but said nothing. Roxanne chatted about inane things just to keep the silence from overwhelming them all.

At the police station he pulled close to the front door. He got out of the car and opened the trunk and pulled out the rolling cart Roxanne had brought with her to carry the papers she brought with her. She had them organized neatly into files and stored in crates that fit nicely on the rolling cart. After he lifted each of them from the trunk he opened the door and helped Mia from the car. He held on to her hand, which was ice-cold as they walked into the station.

Inside they were greeted immediately, "Thank you folks for coming in, I'm Police Chief Joshua David. This here is DA Kole Gray."

Roxanne took the lead. "It's nice to meet you both. This is Mia Gregory, Caiden Marx, and I'm Roxanne Delany. We're happy to be able to have this conversation with you and clear some things up for your department. No matter how old they are."

Chief David nodded, "We're pleased you were willing to come in and talk to us. Please come this way and we'll see what you have."

They were escorted to a conference room and Caiden made sure Mia sat next to him so he could be her support throughout this meeting. Roxanne didn't immediately sit. "I have a plethora of papers to share with you if you'll allow me a few minutes to organize them on the end of the table."

"Absolutely." Chief David replied. "May I offer you coffee or water? I'm afraid it's cop coffee, which is notoriously bad, but it's warm."

Roxanne smiled, "I'd love water please."

Caiden nodded. "I can stand some cop coffee. Mia?"

She smiled to be polite, but it didn't reach her eyes. "No, thank you."

Chief busied himself getting coffee and waters, he kindly set a bottle of water in front of Mia. Caiden thanked him and opened her bottle.

Roxanne finished organizing her papers much as she had them yesterday. "If you're ready, I am."

DA Gray nodded. "I believe we're ready."

"To begin, I want to reiterate why we're here. Sixteen years ago, Mia's mother, Wanda Stewart, was murdered in her home. Mia is a witness to that murder and out of fear of retaliation, she ran away. She's here today to explain what happened. Then we'll talk about any repercussions."

Roxanne smiled kindly and looked at Mia. "Mia, please explain what happened leading up to your mother's murder."

Mia laid her notebook on the table before her. Her fingers shook as she opened to the page where her story started. She cleared her throat. "I'm sorry. I'm so nervous."

Chief David spoke first, "There's no reason to be nervous Ms. Gregory. You're safe here."

Mia nodded and began her recount of her father leaving, her mother and her needing money, Andrea telling her she could make easy money delivering packages. She spoke clearly and succinctly, looking down at her notebook only briefly to remind herself of the events.

At one point her throat dried, and with shaking fingers she took a drink from the bottle of water in front of her, then continued. Caiden kept watching the chief and DA as she told her account of events.

When she finished, Roxanne showed them the medical examiner's report. Then she made them speechless with the list of young women they'd cross-checked with Dominick Nelson's businesses and finally, as if they didn't know, his police record. She further wowed them when she showed them the report, they'd compiled showing Andrea's suicide to a police report that showed Andrea's brother had accused Dominick Nelson of badgering Andrea.

The chief and DA looked over the paperwork in silence, besides the spattering of "Son of a Bitch" and "Unfucking-believable" statements as they read some of the reports.

Finally the DA asked Mia, "Mia what is your purpose for coming in today?"

She took a deep breath and looked him directly in the eye. "I want Dominick Nelson to pay for all he's done to so many people, but mostly I want him to pay for murdering my mother. As an indirect action, my brother now sits in a nursing home, unable to live by himself due to a car accident that was a result of my mother's murder and my disappearance. And, I'm asking you to please not put me in jail for delivering illegal substances. And, I want it known that I didn't kill my mother. I never did drugs. I'm not a bad person. My life has been upended for the last sixteen years as I've hidden myself, terrified that Dominick Nelson would find me and kill me. I don't want to hide anymore."

32

Mia took another drink from her bottle of water and marveled that the shaking had stopped. She watched the chief and the DA look over documents and make notes about certain things. They spoke in respectful terms about her mother and Andrea and the other girls/women who had been abused by Nelson. Finally, DA Gray asked, "Ms. Gregory, may we ask you a few questions?"

"Yes."

She glanced briefly at Roxanne who sat poised and stunningly beautiful, but her eyes didn't miss a thing.

"I want you to know that this is in no way to make you feel as though we don't believe you as to the events as they unfolded, but we'd like to clear a few things up on our end."

"Okay."

"Do you recall what the knife looked like that Nelson held to your mother's throat? Not specific details, but did you recognize it?"

"All I remember was that it had an orange handle."

"Do you recall anything specific about the color?"

Mia shrugged and fidgeted with the label from her water bottle. "It was like a shiny chrome orange. I only remember it because it reflected the light coming in from the window."

Chief David nodded and the DA continued. "Can you tell me anything else about how your mother looked, besides scared? I know this is difficult and we only have a few more questions for you."

Mia swallowed. "She'd been beaten up. Bruises were beginning to form on her face, jaw, and arms. He held her in front of him with the knife at her throat. Her clothing had been torn. She wore a t-shirt and it looked like he'd grabbed a handful of her shirt from the side as she was trying to get away and it ripped. One of her shoes was off."

"One last question. Why didn't you try calling the police?"

"He told me no matter where I went, he'd find me one day. He said the police would never believe me. I was a drug runner."

"But you didn't try to contact your boyfriend, Mr. Marx, or your brother?"

Mia looked at Caiden and she felt sad and embarrassed that she hadn't reached out to him. She left him wondering what had happened all those years.

"Caiden was a promising athlete with a bright future. I didn't want to admit that I'd been stupid and did something illegal. Small towns, they have a way of holding you down and never letting you up. My brother was away at college and I thought he'd be fine. My father took off and I had no intention of trying to find the bastard who put us in this situation to begin with."

"Okay. We won't keep pressing you at this time." The DA looked at Roxanne. "Ms. Delany, what is your proposal?"

"We'll exchange all of this information and the promise that Mia will testify in court as a witness to the murder of her mother for her freedom. No charges for distribution to be brought against Mia, which I do believe the statute of limitations has run, and, of course, the arrest of Dominick Nelson. We have a strong sense that Mia isn't safe in this town until he is off the streets. You have plenty of evidence there to prove that he is a murderer, and he abuses young vulnerable women to get them to traffic his drugs. That's coercion of a minor, contributing to the delinquency of a minor, and a host of other offenses just pertaining to Mia. Couple those with the evidence of trafficking, you have a list of more than forty names there we've identified that you should be able to gather more evidence on his pattern and coercion, plus his rap sheet, you should be able to put him away forever. And, should you be interested in making a deal with Nelson to give up some of his helpers for a lesser sentence, Mia will not testify against him and you will not be allowed our due diligence. You'll be complicit in letting a known murderer run loose in your town, as he has for the past twenty years that we've been able to track. At that point, we'll contact each of these women and their families, as well as

Andrea's family, and we'll bring a class action lawsuit against this police department and county for allowing a man like that to go free. We surely hope it doesn't come to that."

DA Gray didn't flinch and Mia found herself holding her breath. Her future came down to this.

The DA and the chief whispered with each other for a few moments and Mia glanced at Caiden to see how he was dealing with all of this. His hand had remained on the arm of her chair the entire time, to hold on to if she needed him. He looked at her and smiled. "You did great, baby."

She smiled but knew it looked forced.

Finally the DA cleared his throat. "The chief and I are in agreement that the work you've done on this case is stellar and it would have taken us months to compile much of this information. We commend you on your efforts, Ms. Delany. Ms. Gregory, we once again offer our condolences on the murder of your mother, as well as the other family tragedies that have transpired since that date. Dominick Nelson has been a menace in our town for as long as I can remember, and it's been terribly frustrating that we've been unable to pin enough on him to put him away. I can share with you that your description of the knife is extremely helpful to us, as we have that in custody here in our evidence room. It was confiscated from Nelson a few years ago because a witness identified it as the weapon he'd used to scare her. We'll go back now and see if we can find DNA matching that of your mother, which will certainly be the equivalent of the smoking gun. We see no reason to charge you with transporting illegal substances under the circumstances, and as Ms. Delaney has pointed out, the statute has run on that matter, and we apologize again that you and your family fell into the hands of Dominick Nelson under our watch."

Roxanne smiled and leaned forward and wrapped her fingers around Mia's right hand. "Congratulations Mia. You're free."

Mia sat frozen as the words sunk in. The meaning of the words slowly drilled into her subconscious and she felt the heaviness that had weighed her down for sixteen years lift.

Caiden then pulled her in for a hug and her arms wrapped around his waist as much as they could, seated as they were.

"Congratulations, baby."

"Ms. Gregory, you will have to come back to testify but that won't be for a year or so, sooner if we can manage since so much evidence has been compiled for us. Please make sure we have your contact information."

Mia reluctantly pulled away from Caiden and nodded. "I will."

Caiden then stood and shook both men's hands. "When do you think you'll have Nelson arrested? We have people to visit here in town and I want to make sure Mia is safe."

"We'll be sending a squad to his residence as soon as we're finished here. How about I call Ms. Delany when we have him?"

"Yes, thank you."

33

They walked to the car without saying anything. It had been three hours of tension, and to be honest, he was exhausted.

Caiden opened the back door and assisted Mia inside, then opened the trunk and he and Roxanne loaded their evidence. Roxanne told the DA they'd deliver the evidence once the agreement guaranteeing Mia's freedom was signed. Smart lady.

He then opened Roxanne's door and finally climbed into the car himself. He let out a big sigh and Roxanne laughed. "It is a lot of tension, isn't it?"

Roxanne turned in her seat. "Mia, you did a fantastic job today. I know it was difficult, but your freedom is secured and soon they'll have Nelson in custody. Your future is very bright."

He looked in the mirror at Mia and saw her bite her bottom lip. "It's weird but I don't know how to behave. I'm afraid to get excited because it might fall apart and I'll be devastated. I'm afraid not to get excited and it'll all be anti-climactic. I'm sort of numb."

Roxanne nodded. "I understand that. It'll take a bit of time for them to arrest Nelson so the best thing we can do is go back to the hotel and rest. I suspect you didn't sleep well last night, so maybe you'll feel better after a nap. When you wake, hopefully your safety will be that much more secure."

Mia nodded and her eyes captured his in the mirror. He nodded, "I agree with a nap."

Mia smiled at him then turned her head and looked out the window. "Caiden, is it safe for us to drive through town? I'd like to see what it looks like."

He looked at Roxanne, "What do you think?"

"It can't hurt anything."

"I agree. We're in a rented car and as long as we don't get out, we should be fine."

He turned left out of the police station parking lot and navigated another couple of turns to bring them to Main Street. He slowed down just enough that Mia could see things but not so slow as to call attention to them. He looked back often to see her reaction.

"Where's the old hardware store?"

"It's been gone for about eight years now. It burned and old man McGilvry packed up and left town afterwards."

"How about the ice cream...never mind." They hadn't known at the time that Nelson owned it. But they'd spent plenty of time there in high school chatting with friends.

"There's a new cinema at the edge of town. My parents said they felt like they'd been pulled into this century when it opened."

Mia smiled. "How are your parents Caid?"

"They're pretty good. As soon as Nelson is arrested I want to take you there to see them."

Mia smiled, "I'd like that a lot."

He drove to the end of Main Street and turned to drive her past the school they'd shared kisses in. They'd held hands and stolen glances when they'd first started dating. He slowed as they drove passed, and Mia said, "It looks the same."

"It does. Not on the inside though."

"When were you there last?"

"Last year I was home when my nephew, Dillon, had a wrestling match there."

"Who are Dillon's parents?"

"My brother Cord and his wife Deborah."

"Do I know Deborah?"

"No. He met her in college. They fell in love fast and hard and married within a couple of months of dating."

Roxanne laughed, "I know that feeling."

Mia looked up at Roxanne. “How long did you and Hawk date before you married?”

Roxanne laughed. “We didn’t really date. I met him when he broke into my parents’ house after their murder. I was staying there and thought he was a burglar. He thought I was a burglar. We had a row for sure. About a month later, we were married.”

Mia laughed then and Caiden’s heart relaxed a bit. Her solemn mood was lifting. “Wow, that was fast.”

Roxanne nodded and looked out the window.

“Caid?”

“Yeah baby.”

“Will you drive past the nursing home where my brother lives?”

He turned to look into her eyes briefly. “We can’t get out of the car, baby.”

“I know. I just want to see where he is.”

His eyes filled with moisture and he brushed it away with his left hand. “Okay.”

He pulled into a parking lot, turned them around and headed out towards the nursing home at the western edge of town. When he drove close, he looked in the mirror at Mia and smiled.

“This is the home on the left, Mia. It was built fourteen years ago, before that time he was in a home in Hadley.”

Mia stared out the window at the home until they’d driven past. Even then she turned in her seat and looked out the back window until he turned to head back to their hotel. He glanced back at her continuously as tears streamed silently down her cheeks and his heart hurt again.

He pulled into the parking lot at the hotel and quietly opened the door and the trunk, allowing Mia the time she needed to compose herself.

Roxanne joined him by the trunk. "I'm going to go on up. You two take the time you need, and I'll call you when the DA calls me to confirm Nelson is in custody."

He hugged Roxanne. "Thank you so much Roxanne. It was comforting to have you with us and you did an amazing job."

"It was my pleasure. You two get some rest."

Roxanne pulled her cart into the hotel and Caiden opened the back door for Mia. She was swiping her tears away when he climbed in and sat next to her.

"I love you, Mia. Always and forever. We'll get through all of this. Together."

She leaned over and lay her head on his shoulder. "I love you too, Caid. Always and forever. I don't even have the words to express to you how sorry I am for all the years I was away. It was a monumental lapse in judgment on my part in how I handled it."

He wrapped his arm around her shoulders and pulled her close. "You were young and scared and had just witnessed something no one should have to witness. I forgive you."

Her soft sobs filled the silence in the car and he sat and let her get it out. He shed a few tears too for all they had lost. But he was determined to make the years ahead of them all they could be.

34

Caiden's phone ringing woke Mia from a sound sleep. He'd reached over and answered, "Marx."

"Thank God. Thank you for letting us know."

He hung up his phone and turned to see her watching him. "They've arrested Nelson."

She sat up. "Oh my God, I didn't even realize how nervous I'd been about that. I'm so relieved he's in custody. Does that mean we can go out and visit your parents and my brother?"

"Yes. Let me call my parents first. They don't know I'm in town and I don't want to startle them by just showing up."

He scrolled his phone for his mom's number and tapped the 'call' icon. Then he put the call on speaker phone and Mia twisted her fingers together as she sat in the middle of the bed, her legs crossed.

"Caiden, hello honey. How are you?"

"I'm good Mom, how are you and Dad?"

"We're doing well. Did you hear that Dillion took the gold medal in the state wrestling tournament?"

"I didn't hear that. Cord is slacking on keeping me updated."

"They've been running all over the state for Dillon's tournaments."

"I bet they have."

"What's new with you, honey?"

"Mom, I'm in town. I want to come and see you and Dad, and Cord and his family if they're in town. But I'm not alone."

"Oh you never have to ask permission to come home, Caiden. But do tell me, who is with you?"

"Remember Mia Greg...Stewart? From school?"

"Oh that poor girl. I've thought of her so much over the years. Her poor momma and brother."

Caiden reached over and squeezed her hand.

"Mom, Mia is here with me."

Silence on the other end of the phone had Mia staring at Caiden in confusion.

"Mom?"

"Yes dear. I had to sit down. I'm...did you say Mia is with you? How? Where did you find her? How long has she been found?"

"Mom. Let me explain. I found Mia by accident. A friend's husband knew Mia and I tracked her down. We're together now. She's here with me. We want to come and explain what happened to you and Dad."

"Oh dear. Of course, Caiden. Come home."

"We'll be there in about an hour."

"Okay. I'll call Cord. I'm looking forward to seeing you both."

"Me too, Mom. Love you."

He ended the call and scooped her up into his arms. He kissed her lips and held her close. She could feel his breath on her cheeks and close to her ear when he squeezed her. He smelled delicious and she was so grateful to have him here with her.

"Are they going to be mad at me?"

Caiden pulled back and looked into her eyes. His hands framed her face as he said, "I don't know. I have no insight as to anyone's feelings on what happened. But, what happened is in the past. It can't be changed. My family loves me and they may feel a bit over-protective at first because they know how devastated I was when you left. But, they'll also see how happy I am now. And, Mia? I'm happy."

"I'm happy too, Caid. I promise I'll never just run away again. I'll never leave you in the dark about anything again. I'm mature enough now to know better."

He smiled at her and she looked deeply into the ice blue of his eyes as they looked back at her. There was no pretext there. No subterfuge or lies. She saw his soul and it was beautiful.

She kissed his lips, softly and slowly. "Sealed with a kiss."

He chuckled. "Sealed with a kiss. I like that. A lot."

She pulled him close and hugged him hard, then sat back. "I better get ready to see your family."

"You look beautiful just as you are."

Smiling, she stood. "That's sweet of you to say, but I want to look perfect for them. And for you."

She walked to the bathroom and turned on the shower, then poked her head out of the bathroom and crooked her finger at Caiden.

"Now you're talking." He made his way to her in record time.

They enjoyed each other in the shower, touching, loving, soaping, and cleaning. She pushed him down on the bench in the corner of the shower, spread his legs open and backed into him, positioning his cock at her entrance and slowly lowering herself onto him. His hands grasped her hips and helped her up and down on his cock, fast and hard and wet and they both erupted into groans and moans as their orgasms rolled through them. Then they soaped each other up and rinsed and kissed and enjoyed each other's bodies once again. It wasn't the only thing she loved about Caiden, though he was extremely gifted when it came to giving her orgasms. She loved looking at him, talking to him, smelling him, watching him work, watching him with friends. It was all this great big package that she enjoyed the hell out of.

"You're going to exhaust me and I won't have energy to wrestle Dillon." He whispered in her ear.

She laughed, "It sounds like you need to forgo the wrestling with Dillon. He's a state champion now. He'll kick your ass."

Caiden laughed. "Maybe in wrestling, but I can still kick his ass anywhere else. That's a fact."

Mia stepped from the shower and dried off, then padded across the hotel room floor and looked into the closet. Casual but not too casual.

Caiden left the bathroom and chuckled. "Jeans and a nice sweater."

"Isn't that too casual?"

"Nope. You surely remember my parents, Mia. They are as down to earth as they come."

"Yes, but I have a lot of explaining to do so it's important that I look good doing it."

"It's important that you're there in person telling them what happened to a young seventeen-year-old girl after she witnessed her mother's murder."

35

Caiden took Mia's hand and walked to the front door of his parents' house. It was a modest home in Smoky Ridge, WV. All brick, around fourteen-hundred square feet, and they'd lived there all their married life. There were times when it likely felt small. Especially when he and Cord were teenagers and eating them out of house and home. They both had football stuff laying around and they were always on the go. Now though, his parents had plenty of room for just the two of them and they doted on their only grandchild, Dillon. Maybe he'd be able to give them grandchildren one of these days.

Just before they reached the top step, the door opened and his mother stepped out. She was slender, in her late fifties. She often wore jeans or in the summer she wore those cropped short pants that she called capris. Her hair was beginning to gray at the temples, but she kept it neatly cut short and colored a light brown with blonde highlights.

His mom wrapped her arms around his shoulders and gave him a hug like only she could do. He felt her love as she embraced him, her soft voice whispering in his ear, "I've missed you so damned much."

"I missed you too, Mom."

He hugged her back hoping she felt his love in return. When she stepped back he pulled Mia forward by the hand, "Mom, do you remember Mia?"

His mom cupped her face in her hands and looked Mia in the eye. "Oh, you look just the same Mia. You always were such a beautiful young woman." Then his mom hugged Mia. He smiled as he watched them, then his dad stepped out onto the porch.

"I was wondering what the hell was taking so damned long."

Caiden laughed and hugged his dad. "You know Mom. She's got to hug first."

"Damned irritating when a man's waiting to see his son."

Caiden laughed again then said, "Dad, do you remember Mia?"

"I certainly do. Nice to see you again Mia."

"Thank you, sir. It's nice to see you too."

"We're not going to be doing that sir and ma'am crap. I'm Cole or Dad, whichever, but I'm not sir."

Mia laughed. "Okay. I'll start with Cole. If we seem to like each other at the end of our visit, I may switch to Dad."

His dad laughed a hearty laugh and looked him in the eyes. "She's still got sass."

His mom then ushered them into the house. "I have lunch ready and iced tea and Caiden honey do you want a beer? I have that too. Mia, I have wine, or we can scrounge for something else if you don't like it."

His dad looked over at him, "She's been fussing around like this since you called. Driving me damned crazy. I'll be drinking beer!"

Caiden laughed again; my God it felt good to be home.

His mom fussed and dithered and finally his dad said, "Dammit Roseanne, come over here and sit your ass down. Let's hear what they have to say."

His mom carried the last of the snacks she'd prepared to the table and sat. "I just want everyone to be welcomed, full, and happy."

Dad scowled lightly, then looked over at his mom and winked. He tried being a gruff old bird, but he was a softy under all his bluster.

Caiden started the conversation. "I guess I'll just start with how I found Mia and then let Mia tell you what happened to her. Settle in, it'll be a while."

He explained how he'd found her, and his mom beamed. "You always were so smart, Caid."

Then Mia told them what happened before her mom's murder and after. She explained her life, how she'd gotten by, managed to graduate with a GED and go to college, and her job at the paper.

His mom leaned over and took her hand as she spoke, and this time Mia didn't break down completely, though she teared up and stopped to catch herself before she finished telling the story. When she'd finished, the room was quiet; he looked over at Mia and winked.

"We were at the police department this morning. RAPTOR and GHOST pulled together a mountain of information on Dominick Nelson, and Hawk's wife, Roxanne, is here in town and negotiated Mia's freedom for the information. We're now waiting for the DA to draw up the papers then Roxanne will turn over the documents to them. And, we waited to call you until we got word that Nelson had been arrested. We weren't sure he wouldn't try to do something to Mia if he knew she was back in town."

"I'll tell you this, little girl," his dad started, "you've been through a hell of a lot, and I wish you would've felt you could come to us or Caiden. He was devastated when you left. But we understand you weren't thinking clearly and you were scared. But, no more running. Agreed?"

Mia smiled at his father. "Agreed. I've already promised Caiden that I'd never do that again."

His dad nodded and Caiden reached over for Mia's hand and squeezed.

Suddenly the front door burst open and pure reaction caught them as Mia jumped from her chair and ran toward the garage door and Caiden pulled his weapon and pointed toward the front of the house.

"So this is how you greet us after not seeing us in months?" Cord snarled.

Caiden lowered his weapon and holstered it, then looked toward the garage door where Mia had run. She fell against the wall and bent to rest her hands on her knees.

"You okay, baby?"

She nodded and he greeted Cord with the hug he should have gotten and an apology. Deborah stood at the door with her eyes rounded and fear on her face while Dillon stood with a huge grin on his face and said, "That was so cool Uncle Caid. Holy crap you're a fast draw."

36

Caiden slid into bed next to Mia and lay back with a sigh. "I'm still full."

Giggling Mia responded, "Me too. Your mom's a good cook, though. Wow."

He reached out and pulled her close, kissed the top of her head and let out a sigh.

"What happens now Caid? Can we go see my brother tomorrow?"

"I don't see why not. We're still waiting for the DA to get documents to Roxanne. She mentioned that she'll go back home tomorrow if he doesn't get them to her before noon. When she gets them, he can email and she'll look them over before sending them to you."

"What are we going to do?"

"I'll call Emmy tomorrow and see where I have to go for work. But I'd love it if you moved in with me. Live in Lynyrd Station. We have security. A private chef, Sheldon.

A housekeeper, Shioban, she's straight from Ireland and sassy to boot. You can work remotely or find another job."

"Everything's changing so fast."

"Yeah."

She bit her bottom lip. "I'm not comfortable going back to my apartment. I'd be scared all over again there and if you aren't going to be there, I for sure don't want to be there."

"You don't have to decide this minute. But, I want us to be together Mia. I know there will be times I'm gone, but you'll be safe at RAPTOR. The women will all love you. You'll enjoy the kids running around, they keep things lively. And, that's my home base. I'm usually not in the field. I'm cyber team which means I'm normally in the computer lab working. It's just this Dildo case has us all working various jobs. It's a huge trafficking network and we're all determined to bring it down."

Mia thought about his words and swallowed. What the hell was she hesitating for? "If I don't fit in there, is it out of the question to buy a house and live off-site?"

"Of course it's not out of the question. A few of the operatives live in their own homes." He leaned up on his elbow and looked into her eyes. "Why would you think you wouldn't fit in?"

"For the past sixteen years I've been all alone. Just me. It sounds like a lot of activity and it makes me nervous."

He gently brushed the hair off her forehead and brushed the backs of his fingers along her cheek. And she enjoyed how his attention made her feel.

"I want to be with you Mia. You. If living at the compound is stressful, we'll buy a house. I make plenty of money, that isn't an issue. It's just convenient for me to be there. Do you understand?"

"I understand. I just needed to be sure." She ran her fingers along his jaw and enjoyed looking into his blue, blue eyes. "I want to be with you too, Caid. It's all I've ever dreamed of."

He slowly kissed her lips, then her forehead. Then his damned phone rang.

He lay his forehead against hers for a moment and sighed. "Sorry."

She giggled. "Don't be."

She watched the muscles in his back stretch and move as he rolled over and reached for his phone. They were beautiful and firm under the softness of his skin.

"Marx."

He sat up and rested his back against the headboard, pulled his knees up and rested his arm across the top of his knees. "Okay. We can come back with Roxanne tomorrow."

Her heartbeat increased as she thought about living with Caiden. They'd had anything but a normal relationship thus far. And she had to check in with her boss and make arrangements. Then she needed to contact her landlord, and her mind spun with all she needed to do in the coming days. It would perhaps make adjusting to life at RAPTOR a bit easier since she'd have things to do.

"Okay." Caiden ended his call and looked to her but then her phone rang. She laughed at the look on his face before she rolled over and pulled her phone off the other bedside table.

"This is Mia."

"Mia this is Nakita. I just remember something. This man called Jasper Mitchell, he have code name, Skinner66. I hear him talk. He is, what you call it, an Oahu. A money cleaner."

"He laundered money?"

"Yes, that's it. Launder."

"Nakita, thank you for letting me know. This is so helpful."

"I want to help you. You help me."

"Of course and thank you again. Do you need anything right now? Are you safe?"

"Yes. Safe house is good. Police is good too."

"I'm happy to hear it. Stay in touch. I need to pass this information on."

She ended the call and looked at Caiden. "I need to go back and get my notes. I have some here with me, but I do remember one of the women talking about money. Nakita just said that Jasper Mitchell is an Oahu. A money launderer. They usually send large amounts of money overseas and bring it back using various businesses and transactions. They hire themselves out to do this. I'll bet he's been handling the money trail for Dildo and Sergei Romanov."

"That's brilliant. Emmy wanted us to come home, but this may change everything. Let's give her a call back."

Mia listened as Caiden explained the Oahu and that she had some notes in Vegas. She told him to go back to Vegas, get her notes and pack things up. Donovan was now on the trail of Skinner66 but would need back-up. Piper was backing up Creed, so he was needed.

He ended his call with Emmy and said, "Mia, we're headed to Vegas in the morning. O-seven hundred hours. I promised you a trip to see your brother. I'm sorry."

"It's okay. It will be a shock to him. I think what I'll start with is a phone call to my Aunt Rebecca and see what she thinks is the best way to handle letting Ashton know about me."

He leaned forward and kissed her lips. "You're smart."

She shook her head. "Maybe just weary of the whole sordid tale of my past and needing a break from retelling it again tomorrow. Maybe cowardice. Maybe avoidance."

"Definitely smart. Don't sell yourself short."

37

The sun had been up a couple of hours as the three of them boarded the plane. They'd drop Roxanne off in Lynyrd Station then head to Vegas. While they flew, Mia made a list of the things she needed to do, then sent emails to people she needed to contact. Caiden let her be while he worked on his laptop. Deacon emailed a few times about Skinner66 and sent some leads. Caiden followed up with those leads, searching through the networks that RAPTOR had amassed about Oahus and some of their patterns.

His computer pinged a location for an Oahu who had regular contact with Russia. The network was complicated, the spiderweb it weaved confusing, and he had no doubt that was done on purpose. Keep authorities running in circles to avoid getting caught. He kept notes, added locations and then found a web that kept leading back to the same place.

He emailed Deacon.

To: Deacon Smythe

From: Caiden Marx

Time: 07:48 a.m.

RAPTOR OAHU INVESTIGATION

Deac,

Found a string that leads from several different locations in Florida to several locations in Russia. All are within the first five days of each month. I'm in the air now, and don't have full access to the server. Will you check these dates to shipments of containers that came into and left the US from Russia?

Caiden

He sent his email and lay his head back to close his eyes. Mia was right, things were changing fast. His email pinged and he lifted his head and opened his laptop.

To: Caiden Marx

From: Deacon Smythe

Time: 08:17 a.m.

RAPTOR OAHU INVESTIGATION

Caid,

Great thought on the leads. Comparing the shipments of containers to the US, one day later a shipment of money was sent, from Florida, via an Oahu to Russia. One day after a container arrived in Russia, a payment was sent to an Oahu in Florida. These transactions all take place within the first five days of each month. I've only compared the first few months of this year, but we'll be pulling all of this together to track just how long this has been going on.

Deacon

He glanced at Mia, who was typing away on her laptop. He didn't want to bother her so he sent a reply to Deacon.

To: Deacon Smythe

From: Caiden Marx

Time: 08:22 a.m.

RAPTOR OAHU INVESTIGATION

Deac,

Anywhere on that trace do you see Skinner66? I just wondered if he's been able to embed his identity into the wire so he can search but hid it from the trace itself. The receiver would only see some other code name associated with him. For instance, when a payment came into Container World for payment of the cargo from Russia, was there someone else listed as the payor? Obviously they wouldn't use their actual names, but some code or something?"

Caiden

Now he couldn't rest. His mind was racing, wondering how they'd managed to send payment back and forth and who was organizing those payments and for whom. He wanted the whom in this scenario. Then he turned to Mia. "Hey, hate to bother you, but I have a question."

She stopped typing and looked over at him. "Okay."

"When you delivered the packages for Nelson, were you given anything to prove you had delivered it? A note? An envelope? Some proof that it had been delivered? Otherwise how would Nelson know you'd actually delivered the package?"

"There was an envelope taped on the package that the recipient had to pull off in front of me. He always said the same thing. 'The timer is on.'"

"Do you know what that means?"

"No. Nelson asked me when I was finished what the recipient said. "I delivered three packages to three different people and they all said that. I never questioned it." Mia took a deep breath as the light dawned. "They had a code. I was also sending back verification that the package had been delivered. But, what did it mean that the timer is on?"

"I'll bet there was a time frame the recipient had for selling the drugs. If there had been a problem there was likely another code used."

He turned to Roxanne who sat across the aisle and back one row. "Roxanne. Have you ever heard of this?" He explained the coded messages.

Roxanne shook her head. "No, but I'll tell the chief and the DA to make sure they ask that question when they interview the other people I'll be giving them."

Mia clicked her mouse a few times and began typing again. "Caiden, the Oahu is a great story angle. Mind if I write about it?"

"Of course not. Just don't publish it until we have this case wrapped up. You'll let them in on the direction of our investigation."

"I wouldn't do that to you all."

She kept typing and Therese announced over the intercom that they'd be landing soon in Lynyrd Station.

Caiden looked at Roxanne and smiled. "Home sweet home. Tell everyone hello from us."

"I will. I hope you'll be home soon to say it yourselves."

The plane descended, landed, and Roxanne walked off. They'd refuel and be back in the air within a few minutes.

His mind raced; they were on to something for sure. Dildo had a code he was using.

His computer chimed an email and he opened it.

To: Caiden Marx

From: Deacon Smythe

Time: 09:03 a.m.

RAPTOR OAHU INVESTIGATION

Caid,

He embedded a code in each transaction. S66. That has to mean Skinner66. What do you think? I'll send you the embedded details so you can decipher for yourself.

Deacon

38

It was exciting watching Caiden work. When they were on to something he moved quickly. His throat pulsed as his heart rate increased and due to his lung issues, his breathing got raspy. She didn't even have to look at him to know they were closing in on something, and by proxy, she was excited too. All the women who had been abused by this disgusting group would feel thousands of times better knowing they were off the streets.

She tried to focus on her own writing. She still owed an article to her editor and she had to chat with him about working remotely. Or not at all, depending on how he reacted to her working remotely. Ideas percolated in her brain about what she'd do if her editor told her to take a hike. She almost hoped for that to be the case. She'd start her own online magazine and include her articles from over the years to get it going. All the interviews she'd done of the women who were survivors of sex trafficking, she'd done on her own time. They were her articles picked up by media outlets around the globe. She could monetize her magazine and approach businesses to pay for ads.

Therese announced, "Please fasten your seatbelts and prepare for takeoff."

The next time they landed in Lynyrd Station, she'd be moving here. Her stomach twisted a bit at the thought of starting all over. But then again, it didn't, in a way. It would be nice to have a place to actually live. She hadn't really lived anywhere in sixteen years. By that she meant, she hadn't LIVED. She'd survived and kept putting one foot in front of the other, but that was the extent of it. She avoided relationships other than casual. She didn't go out for drinks after work because she was afraid someone would drug her and haul her back to Nelson. She didn't go to birthday parties, baby showers of co-workers, retirement parties at work, none of them, all for the same reason.

Their flight took off and while Caiden sat next to her, they were both in their own headspace. But it was comforting to sit next to him, relaxed and safe.

His phone rang and he pulled it from his pocket.

"Marx."

He glanced at her then stared straight ahead and her stomach twisted.

"Thank you. I'll tell her to watch for the email. Thanks Roxanne."

He smiled. "Your freedom is about to be official. Roxanne has received the documents from the DA outlining the agreement to supply them with the evidence we've compiled in exchange for your freedom and agreement to testify against Nelson. She's going to look it over and make sure it's written as it needs to be and then she'll send it over to you. She said to give her an hour."

"Wow. That's fantastic. I'll watch for it."

"She also said someone within the organization, meaning either GHOST or RAPTOR, has located your Aunt Rebecca's contact information and will forward that to you also."

She swallowed, and her heart raced at the thought of speaking to her aunt after so many years. Always the first thought was that they'd be so mad at her. And they had the right to be. But she dreaded the tongue lashing and the guilt. Always the guilt.

But she wanted to see Ashton again. She wanted to be able to see him regularly. Maybe one day he'd agree to move to Indiana, close to where she lived so they could visit regularly. That was likely way down the line though, and she didn't want to get too far ahead of herself. One step at a time.

She turned her head and stared out the window at the fluffiness of the clouds under them and the shapes they made. When she and Ashton were young, they'd lay in the front yard and point out shapes and animals they'd see in the clouds, it had been such a fun time for them. Especially when the clouds were super fluffy and the plethora of shapes, animals, and even faces they found made them laugh.

Therese's voice sounded once again over the speakers, "Please prepare for landing."

She glanced at Caiden who smiled at her. "You fell asleep." He leaned in and kissed her lips softly. "I love watching you sleep."

"Did my mouth hang open?"

He chuckled. "No, but you drooled."

"I did not." But just to make sure she touched her chin and looked down at her shirt to check. Caiden laughed and she socked him in the arm.

"Also, you got your email from Roxanne. She texted to let me know she sent it and I told her you'd fallen asleep. You can read it when we get to the hotel."

"Okay. Then what?"

"We're dropping our things off at the hotel, giving you time to read through the Agreement with Smoky Ridge County, and then we'll go to your apartment and pack your things. Therese will wait with the plane and we'll put everything on board for her to fly back."

"Wow, that's really nice of her."

Caiden chuckled. "She has to fly back either way, and this will give her a chance to eat lunch and relax a bit before flying back."

"Makes sense."

"I've emailed my boss. I've emailed my landlord. And, once I sign the documents from the DA, I'll email my aunt. It's all starting to feel real. Sort of."

Caiden squeezed her hand. "I couldn't be happier."

Mia smiled and braced herself when the plane touched the ground.

39

The amazing Piper Roman had brought boxes, paper for wrapping dishes, and bags to put clothing in so they didn't get wet. "They're used, but in good shape. I used them when I moved my stuff here and Royce tells me when he's finished playing football, we'll hire movers to move us wherever we're going."

"Do you know where that is, Pipes?"

"I'm hoping back to Lynyrd Station. That's the last conversation we've had about it. I sort of miss you jerks."

Caiden laughed. "Yeah, we miss being called jerks every day."

Piper just shrugged.

Mia's phone rang and he half listened to the conversation. "Okay. Come on up to the third floor. I'll open the door and wait there for you."

She looked over in his direction. "Movers are here."

They had the boxes stacked in the living room, the bed was taken apart, and basically the place looked empty. Mia looked around and he couldn't quite tell what the expression on her face was.

"You okay?"

She turned to face him, a soft smile on her face. "Yeah."

"Is this hard?"

She looked around again, the dark ponytail on the top of her head swished side to side as she turned her head.

"I guess, just a bit. It took me three years to feel somewhat safe here. Then, I used this place as my safe space where I'd come and hide after work, many times while my work friends were out partying and having fun. I came back here and wrote my articles or interviewed women on the phone. Most recently it hasn't been my safe space and still I have these stupid mixed feelings about leaving it."

Caiden stepped over to her and wrapped her in his arms. He kissed the top of her head and held her. "You're entitled to feel however you feel. You don't have to understand it or agree with how you feel, it just is."

She looked up into his eyes and smiled, "Thank you for understanding."

The elevator chimed and Piper interrupted, "I'll get them here. You two are too mushy to watch anyway."

Caiden laughed. "At least she didn't call us jerks."

Mia laughed and he felt better. Lighter, happy. They were going to be together. Eventually.

The movers walked into the apartment and without saying anything started loading boxes up onto a cart to be taken to a truck, which would then be taken to the plane.

He texted Therese and told her the apartment was now being loaded to the truck, received a thumbs-up and helped load up carts of boxes. She didn't have much and it wouldn't be more than three loads down in the elevator, so they'd go on to her office and grab the recorder, then back to the hotel.

He felt his phone buzz and pulled it from his pocket. A text from Deacon: "Call me."

He stepped away from the noise in the living room, into Mia's bedroom and called Deacon.

"Hey. Listen, Dildo is still in Vegas."

"How do you know?"

"I kept the tracking information on his phone and figured out another way to track him by tapping into his GPS."

"Fuck, that's brilliant."

"Right, but this is the thing. He's watching you. He's a block away, and he keeps walking past the building. I think he's trying to figure out what's going on and timing it just right to get inside."

"We have movers here now moving Mia's things out."

"I wouldn't let those guys out of my sight if I were you. He'll either pay one of them or knock one of them out and replace them to get to her."

"Thanks. You keep watching him. We're on it here."

"Roger."

"Pipes, Mia, quick word."

Both women walked to him across the room and he quietly shared what Deacon had just told him.

"So, one of us, meaning me or Piper, will go down with these guys every time they get in the elevator and stand guard. I'll call Creed right now and get him here."

Piper nodded. "I'm on it. First time down."

She walked over to the movers and stepped in front of the door to the hall, when they were ready to go down to the truck she looked in, caught his eye and nodded. Caiden then walked to the door and locked it. He went to the window and looked down to see if he could see Dildo, and Mia began scrounging in a box.

"What are you looking for?"

"More ammo."

"Hey," he was going to tell her not to bother, but then thought better of it. "Never mind. Good idea."

Mia scrounged till she found her ammo stash, which she tucked in her back pocket, already loaded in a magazine. Caiden grinned but continued to look out the window without being seen.

It took around fifteen minutes and a knock on the door had him running to see who it was. He held his hand up to Mia asking her to stay in the back of the apartment, then looked through the peephole to see Creed.

He opened the door and let his teammate inside then shared the plan.

Creed said, "Let's do this. You and Mia go down to the parking garage and head to her office then the hotel. I'll stay here, and Piper and I will each take turns watching the movers and keeping an eye out for Dildo. He doesn't want her stuff, he wants Mia. If she isn't here, it helps our position."

"Good plan."

He looked at Mia. "Are you on board with that?"

"Yes."

"Thanks Creed. I'll let Deacon know to watch and make sure Dildo doesn't follow us."

"I'll do it, you just get down to the parking garage without being seen."

Caiden looked at Mia and she walked to his side. "Stay by me at all times. Only do what I say until we're safe."

"Okay."

He opened the door and looked down the hall. The stairs were at the far end of the hall and it was clear. He stepped out and waited for Mia to join him, then walked as naturally as possible to the stairs. Once they reached the top, he opened the door and looked down the stairs for anyone lurking inside.

Glancing back at Mia, he nodded and they descended the steps at an even pace. His heart rate increased as they neared the garage, mostly because one wrong move right now would put Mia in danger and he couldn't forgive himself if he did that. They passed the second-floor door and kept moving to the first-floor door. He glanced back at Mia and saw her face set firmly, her eyes rounded, and her breathing was rapid.

He held up his forefinger for one more floor and they crept down to the parking garage area. At the bottom of the steps he opened the door and looked into the garage. This is where it was tricky. With all the cars parked inside it was difficult to tell if someone was hiding behind a car. His rented SUV was only four cars from the door and he stepped to the wall and looked down the row of cars not seeing anyone hiding there. He also saw a decent sized path to the vehicle by walking along the wall.

He whispered to Mia. "We're going to walk along the wall."

She nodded, and he quietly pulled the keys to the car out of his pocket, so he had the fob in his left hand. Thumb on the unlock button they edged their way toward the SUV, as quiet as they could be. They reached the passenger side of the SUV first and Caiden opened the door, which beeped and made a noise, then quickly ushered Mia inside. He ran around the back of the SUV and climbed in the driver's seat.

His phone buzzed in his pocket, but he didn't want to take the time to answer, so he started the vehicle and began to back out when his phone buzzed again. He tugged it from his pocket and handed it to Mia. "See who that is please."

"Caiden's phone."

He backed out and put the vehicle in gear when Mia yelled. "He's here. Right..."

She twisted her head and yelled. "Behind us."

Caiden yelled, "Get down!"

He slammed the SUV into reverse and stepped on the gas. A thud hit the back of the SUV, then Caiden switched gears and took off out of the garage. He looked in his mirror only once to see someone, presumably Dildo moving around and trying to sit up.

"Call Creed."

Mia fumbled nervously with his phone but found his contacts and Creed's number.

"Creed, we hit him. Dildo, he's in the garage."

Mia turned her head and looked out the back window as Caiden turned the corner and out into the street.

"I'll see if I can get him."

40

Mia felt like she was going to throw up. “Why is he after me? All I’ve done is write the story on the women.”

“He’s a fucked-up mess Mia. He’s vengeful and he managed to find you. He might also think he can get you to tell him where the women are.”

“Fuck.”

She tried breathing easy as Caiden carefully drove through traffic toward her office. She just wanted to get out of Vegas all together.

She turned to him, “Any chance I can get on the plane with my stuff?”

He glanced at her a couple of times, watching the road carefully. “I’ll call Emmy.”

Caiden’s phone rang and Mia was still hanging on to it. She glanced down to see whose name was on the screen.

"It's Creed."

"Can you answer it?"

She tapped the answer icon and the speaker icon. "Hi Creed, I have you on speaker so Caiden can hear."

"Caid, he was gone when I got down there. Do you know how badly he was hurt?"

"Negative. I saw him trying to get up, that was it, we turned onto the street and I couldn't see anymore."

"Okay. I didn't see blood. I'm not sure how badly he's been hurt. I'll have Deacon track him and we'll watch where he goes."

"Roger that."

Creed ended the call and Mia looked over at him. "Didn't Emmy tell you to get him if you saw him? Won't you get in trouble?"

"She did. But, I wasn't going to put you in harm's way. We'll get him."

"Caiden..."

"No, Mia. No. You come first. I know Emmy wants Dildo. We all do. But not at the risk of one of our own."

She sat back in the seat and her head hurt with all the stuff running through it. For so long, she'd been hiding from one person. Never in her wildest dreams would she have thought she needed to worry about someone besides Dominick Nelson. She inhaled deeply and tried holding her breath for ten seconds, then let it out while silently counting to ten to calm herself.

Caiden pulled up to her newspaper building and her heart raced once again. So much for the breathing exercise.

"Do you have a secure garage here?"

"Yes. Pull up to that driveway ahead and turn right. It'll circle us around the building and down to the garage."

Caiden's phone rang again and he grabbed it from her hands and answered. "Marx."

He tapped the speaker icon so he could navigate the driveway and set his phone in the cup holder.

"It's Deacon. So, there's a whole shit show going on now. Emmy's calling everyone back to headquarters. Except Piper. She'll call in. And, Diego, Falcon, and I will be flying out to Florida."

"What the hell is going on?"

"So that Oahu tracking we've been doing. Suddenly there's shit going on. Apparently the Russian tried pulling his money back from Florida because he stopped his shipment of women. The internet is blowing up, at least the tracking we're doing. It appears Florida, which we assume is Dildo's Oahu, is trying to hang on to the money and there was just a murder outside of the location we've now identified as one where the Oahu is based out of. I can see from the cameras across the street what's happening. It's gangland shit going on."

"But Dildo is here."

"Right. I think he was making one last attempt to get to Mia. My guess is he wanted her to tell him where the women were so he could keep the money and send them over. At least the American women."

"Can you see him through the tracker?"

"He looks like he's headed to the airport."

"No shit."

Caiden looked over at her, then turned down to the parking garage.

"So, Emmy wants us back at headquarters?"

"You and Creed are to come back. Of course bring Mia if she's coming to live here. Diego, Falcon, and I are heading out as soon as Therese gets to the airport. We need you on the computers and Creed needs to rest up and get ready in case he's called in again. For all we know right now, whatever was going on in Vegas is likely finished."

"Roger that, Deacon. We're just now heading to Mia's newspaper to box up her things, then we'll pick up Creed and head to the airport."

"Roger. I'll let him know."

Caiden found a parking spot as close to the elevator as he could. They stepped in and he held her hand. Her mind was a mess right now and all she wanted to do was get on the plane and get to a safe place. She'd likely not sleep well here anyway.

The elevator stopped on the fourth floor and they stepped off.

"My desk is over to the right."

A few people said hi to her and Mia always said hi back,

she didn't want to stop and explain. Her editor, Gabriel Francisco's door was closed so she started cleaning out her desk. She found a box next to the copy machine where reams of paper had been used, and as usual no one bothered to discard the empty box. Worked for her.

Just as she had the last of her belongings packed up, Gabriel's door opened. He looked directly across the room at her and nodded.

"Come on in."

Mia looked up at Caiden. "Do you want to wait in the car?"

"No. I'm not leaving you up here. I'll either go in with you or wait here. You pick."

"Come in with me."

She introduced Gabriel to Caiden, told her story as quickly as she could, said she was still being stalked and needed to get out of town, and asked if she could work remotely. All in a matter of a few minutes. Gabriel stared at her, mouth agape, for a long time before he finally shook his head to bring his brain back around and said, "Of course you can work remotely."

He then ran his hands down his face and said, "I'm shocked, Mia. I never knew you'd gone through all of that. You've been a stellar employee and never any trouble. I'm so very sorry for all you've gone through."

She smiled at Gabriel. "You've always been a great editor to work for and I thank you for that. Thank you for giving this newbie a chance."

She promised to submit her next article on time. Gabriel said he'd email her an assignment in the morning and Mia and Caiden left the building as quickly as they could. She didn't breathe easy until they stepped on the plane.

41

Caiden leaned over the bed and kissed Mia. She rolled over and smiled. Looked at his clothes and sat up.

"Where are you going?"

"I have a meeting with the team. Shelby, Diego's wife, will be down here in a half hour to show you around and introduce you to the other wives and kids. When our meeting ends, I'll introduce you to my teammates who are here. Deal?"

"You arranged all of this while I was sleeping?"

He chuckled. "You were sleeping soundly and you needed it. And I've been awake for a couple of hours. So, yes." He kissed her again. "I love you."

As he walked toward the door she said, "I love you too."

There, he needed to hear that. He grinned as he made his way downstairs.

Waving his keycard in front of the electronic elevator access pad, the doors swished silently open and he stepped inside. It had been a few weeks since he'd been home, and it felt good to be back here once again. And, he was here with Mia. Bonus.

Once the elevator doors opened in the lower level, Caiden walked to the conference room and greeted his teammates who were in attendance. Emmy, Creed, Charly, Donovan.

"Bout time you got back, slacker." Donovan chided.

"Vegas, baby." Caiden responded.

Creed laughed and Charly giggled. "I'm looking forward to meeting Mia."

Caiden smiled. "She's gonna love you."

Emmy limped to the table, "Okay, Piper are you on?"

"Yes. Morning, everyone."

They all greeted Piper then Emmy continued, "Falcon, Diego, and Deacon, are you on?"

"Yes, we're here," Falcon answered.

"Okay, Caiden tell us what you found this morning and catch us up to speed on where we're at with Dildo and the Russians."

"So, throughout the night there was more chatter on the internet between the Russians and our Florida person. But, here's what I've managed to track, the Oahu is Jasper Mitchell. Remember his name? One of the women told Mia he was the driver Dildo, Dawson, and Haywood were waiting for with the American women. He works with

Dildo. He's the money man. Dildo is the scum who rounds up the women. Jasper is the person Nadia, the Russian contact speaks with. It's been chatter between Nadia and Jasper that I've intercepted. She's pissed off and sent the killers to the office where Jasper works. Which is really a little room behind a laundromat. They killed someone, we aren't sure how they belong, but it was more of a warning. Nadia knows she won't get her money if she kills Jasper. Nadia is Sergei Romanov's Oahu."

"That's fantastic work, Caiden."

"Actually Deacon found the chatter channel. Teamwork."

Emmy then directed the conversation to Diego and Falcon. "What are you two doing today?"

Diego answered first. "We're heading to the office we believe Jasper is working out of and we're hoping to spot Dildo in the area."

"Is he there?"

Caiden responded. "We've tracked him to Florida. South Miami specifically."

"Fantastic. Falcon and Diego, how far is that from where you're at?"

Diego responded. "We're in North Miami. In light traffic we can be in South Miami in an hour."

"Okay. So, let's listen to the chatter, watch the tracking on Dildo. See if we can manage to get eyes on Jasper so we know what he looks like and capture these bastards."

Their meeting disbanded and Emmy looked at him. "Glad to have you back Caiden. I'm looking forward to meeting

Mia."

"Thanks Emmy. If we can get things wrapped up here, I did promise to take her back to see her brother. We didn't manage it when we were there before."

"I think that's a great idea."

Caiden went to the computer and put his headset on. Deacon had done a great job of organizing all he needed to know. A little popup on his screen showed; it was a private message from Piper.

"I'm glad you're back at the compound. Is Mia alright?"

"Yes, thank you for asking. She started breathing normally once we were up in the air."

"Happy to hear it. I'm on this side watching from afar. I'll relieve you at the computer in a few hours. Holler if you need anything."

"Thanks, Pipes."

Caiden looked over Deacon's notes and logged into the tracking system and the chatter system to continue to monitor chats and movement.

After listening for a while the chatter seemed to die down, and now had been silent for the past forty-five minutes. Caiden stood and stretched and texted Mia.

"Hey there. What are you doing?"

"Shelby and I are playing in the yard with the kids."

"Are you good?"

"Yes. Relaxed. Everyone has been very nice."

"See you soon. Piper will relieve me in about an hour."

"Love you. See you soon."

Caiden smiled as he set his phone in the charging cradle on his desk. He'd call his parents and his brother later today. They would need to know they were safe and Mia was with him.

Then, he'd talk to Mia about their living arrangements. So many decisions to make and of course, she was going to need to prepare for Nelson's trial. Roxanne couldn't try Dominick's case in West Virginia, but she said she'd stay in contact with the DA and help him throughout the trial. That made both Mia and him feel so much better.

The door opened and Mia and Charly walked in.

"Hey there."

"I brought this girl down to see where we keep you chained to the desk while you're working."

"Thanks Charly." He smiled at Mia. "Was she nice to you? She can be a sass."

Mia laughed. "She was incredibly nice. She wouldn't even tell stories on you."

"There aren't any stories to tell. So..."

Charly laughed. "Not true Caid, but I didn't want to scare her away the first day."

"Ouch."

Both women laughed and Caiden looked around. "Well let me show you our offices and introduce you to Emmy."

42

Her first day at RAPTOR had been interesting. She'd met those who were there, and she managed to meet Yvette and Isabella from GHOST. Both formidable women and Mia felt incredibly at home with them. But, as Caiden showered, it was time to write an email to her Aunt Rebecca.

She sat on the sofa in Caiden's apartment, her laptop in front of her and her stomach in her throat. How did one suddenly explain, hey guess what? I'm not dead?

To: Rebecca Hamilton

From: Mia Gregory (Stewart)

Time: 3:05 p.m.

Dear Aunt Rebecca,

I know this email will come as a great surprise to you and I apologize for that. I honestly don't know how to make this less shocking or less awkward.

Obviously, I'm writing this email which means I am alive. I have been living and hiding in Las Vegas since Mom's murder. Most recently, I've been working with local authorities to bring the man who murdered Mom to justice. He has now been arrested which has helped me feel safe enough to come out of hiding.

If you can find it in your heart to speak with me, I would like to tell you what happened and reconnect with you. There will be a trial coming soon, and I'll need to testify as the only witness to Mom's murder. I'd like for you to know the facts before you begin hearing about the salacious events as the press will no doubt make them seem. I can say that because I've been a reporter for the past eight years.

I've attached a photo of me, taken just this past year, so you can see it is actually me and not someone pretending.

Yours Very Truly,

Mia

She hit send and sat back wondering how long it would take for Aunt Rebecca to respond or if she would.

Caiden walked out of the bathroom; the fresh aroma of shower soap filled the air and his handsome face was a sight to see. He'd been working today in the same building, but she still missed him. He slipped on jeans and pulled socks from a drawer.

"Hey, are you alright?"

She smiled. "Yeah. I finally sent Aunt Rebecca an email. For someone who writes for a living, I don't think I did my best work. But, honestly, I'd prefer to speak with her or see her face-to-face when I have to tell her everything. So, I made it brief and now I'm second-guessing everything I wrote."

Caiden slipped a t-shirt over his sexy body and sat next to her, his socks hanging from his fingers.

"You worry too much. Of course she'll want you to prove you are who you say you are, and I've spoken to Emmy about going back to West Virginia so you can see your brother. We should be able to head out of town in a day or two."

She smiled at him. So supportive and handsome to boot. "I'm so lucky to have you in my life, Caid."

He grinned and leaned forward, touching his lips to hers. "I'm the lucky one."

"Hmm, doubtful, but just the same, I'm happy to be here with you."

"Me too." He tugged his socks on and she once again enjoyed how his muscles played as he moved. "So tell me, who did you meet today?"

She sighed, "Let's see. I met Isi and Yvette, and Yvette and Axel's son Aidyn. They were all so easy to talk to and Aidyn is a great kid. I met Sheldon, who is simply an amazing cook, but at first meeting I thought maybe he was too gruff. Then Diego and Shelby's kids came running in after school and Sheldon melted like butter. He had special snacks for the kids and joked with them and I knew he was a softy inside. I met Shioban briefly, she was busy, and I didn't want to bother her. And of course,

Charly, Emmy, oh and Roxanne introduced me to Hawk. They are stunning together."

He chuckled again. "Yeah, I guess."

She softly punched him in the arm. "You guess. Sheesh why is it so hard for guys to admit stuff like that?"

He shrugged. "What do you want to do tonight?"

"What would you be doing if I weren't here?"

Caiden shrugged. "Watching a movie, reading, or working out. We don't have group things we do here and if we're in the mood for company, we watch television in the formal living room, or go down to the lower level and see who's hanging around."

"Okay. I wouldn't mind watching a movie downstairs if it means I'll meet more of your friends."

"Okay. But for the time being, I just need to run downstairs for about a half hour and make sure Piper is connected to our chatter channel. Are you alright here for a few more minutes?"

She giggled. "I'm fine."

He kissed her lips then turned and left the room.

Her phone buzzed and she looked at it to see that she'd received an email from her Aunt Rebecca. Her heart pounded and her hands shook. She sat like a stone on the sofa and swallowed compulsively until she could manage the courage to actually read it.

She blew out a few breaths and closed her eyes, then she sent up a silent prayer that her aunt was happier she was still alive than she was angry with her.

Finally getting her emotions somewhat under control, Mia tapped on the email and began to read.

43

Caiden logged in to his computer and PM'd Piper.

Caiden: "All good?"

Piper: "I'm intercepting something weird on the chatter channel. It's a clicking sound and I think it's someone trying to hack in."

Caiden checked the channel himself and listened briefly.

Caiden: "I hear it too."

Piper: "Can you see where it's coming from?"

Caiden typed into his keyboard and tried using the code they'd developed to see if he could track this new hacker.

Caiden: "I'm trying to track now."

As he loaded the map on his computer screen, he also added the overlay of the screen with the glowing dots on it. These dots were the location origins of the people who were on this chatter. Until last night, there'd only been two blue dots. Now there was a third one and it was dangerously close to Falcon, Deacon, and Diego.

Caiden: "Pipes, it's coming from Florida."

Piper: "Does Deacon have the ability to patch in remotely and check it out for himself?"

Caiden: "He has limited ability, but I'll alert him and see if he can hear anything different from what I'm hearing."

Piper: "That's great. I'll try a few things from my end here to see if I can get any location pinpoints or visuals."

Caiden: "Roger."

Caiden then contacted Deacon by telephone.

"Smythe."

"Hey Deac. It looks like we have a hacker trying to tap into our chatter channel. Do you have ability to see that from your location? The hacker appears to be in Florida. Not sure if Jasper or Nadia have someone else trying to hack in or if we have a kid in his mom's basement thinking it's funny."

"Send me the IP once you have it and I'll see if I can locate it from here."

Caiden grabbed the IP the next time the hacker tried getting in and sent it to Deacon. He let Piper know what they were doing, and he opened up their group chat so they were all in the loop.

Caiden: "Just sent hacker IP to Deacon."

Deacon: "Got it."

Caiden watched as the lights flashed and blipped. Basically they could see the locations of where the hackers were located, but until they logged on the lights were dim. Once the hacker logged on the lights glowed. Right now, Jasper and their new hacker were on.

Piper: "I've got a visual of Jasper. Sending it over to you now."

Soon a photograph appeared on the screen, a male, with blond hair in need of a cut, wearing a bulky jacket. The background of the picture looked to be a dimly lit, depressing space, with cluttered shelves behind him and a full wastebasket in the far-right corner.

Piper: "He looks to be in his forties. I'm trying to dig up any trail of Jasper. Might not be his real name."

Caiden: "I've seen his picture before Pipes. Run a scan of the Container World rescue. He was there."

Deacon: "He was. He's in the frames just before you were rescued, Pipes. He was the driver Dawson, Haywood, and Dildo were waiting for. He stopped at the gate and spoke to Jason LeBeau, the asshole who supposedly inspected the containers. Jasper was there to see which containers held the women and he was going to take the Russian women and disperse them to their new owners."

Piper: "I wonder if that gross Deke Spivey, the pimp I met at Bobby Lee Slater's house was one of the new owners? I'm checking into that."

Caiden: "You might be able to get that information from Bobby Lee. He was being blackmailed by Spivey. He may want to make another deal to keep his ass out of prison."

Piper: "Great idea. I'll call the DA now."

Caiden blew up the picture of Jasper and stared at his face. He wanted to memorize this asshole. Then another picture popped on and off his screen. Like it was a bad connection and the photo couldn't completely populate.

Deacon: "When Piper initiated the camera to get Jasper's photo, she must have also snagged our new hacker in the mix. I think that's his picture trying to populate."

Caiden: "I'll try to grab it when it pops up."

He waited with his finger on his mouse for that picture to show up. Several times he'd missed it, his frustration growing. Finally he managed to get a partial picture of...holy shit it was a her. All he could make out was reddish hair and she looked small.

Deacon: "That's our hacker? She looks twelve."

Caiden: "Like you said, kid in her mom's basement."

Deacon: "Fuck, just what we need is some kid screwing up our investigation. I'm going to try and grab a location on this kid."

Caiden continued trying to capture a good photo of the girl and then another light popped onto his screen. He watched where this new green light was and noted that it was within about sixty miles or so of the hacker.

Caiden: "Deacon is that green dot you?"

Deacon: "Yes."

Caiden: "Do you see how close you are to our hacker?"

Deacon: "Affirmative. Trying to capture the exact location."

Caiden watched as the lights came on and then went off and just as he thought he'd snagged her picture, her light went off completely. "Fuck."

Deacon: "Fuck."

Caiden: "My words exactly."

Piper: "DA is going to work on Bobby Lee."

Caiden stood and stretched. Emmy entered the conference room and smiled. "Long day for you."

"It is. We're getting close Emmy."

"I've been watching on my phone. We're going to get that fucker."

Caiden chuckled. Emmy was fierce.

She glanced at him. "Go spend time with Mia, Caid. You've been at it too long and you'll get fatigued."

44

To: Mia Gregory (Stewart)

From: Rebecca Hamilton

Time: 3:24 p.m.

Dear Mia,

I can't tell you what a shock it was to read your email and I'll be honest and tell you now that I'm still sitting in disbelief. I'd very much like to video chat with you so we can see each other and I'd very much like to know what happened to my sister and to you.

I don't know if you've heard about Ashton and his accident, I would like to discuss this with you as well. Things haven't been the same since that awful day, our lives have all been irreparably altered.

If you are open to having a video conference with me, please let me know and I'll set it all up through my office.

Yours truly,

Rebecca

Mia sat back and held her hand over her heart. It beat so hard it almost hurt. Tears flooded her eyes and she couldn't take a deep breath. Lifting her laptop and moving it next to her, she scooted to the edge of the sofa and waited to make sure her legs would hold her up if she dared to move.

The door opened and Caiden walked in. Immediately his face was washed in concern. "What happened? Are you alright?"

She could only nod. Her lips parted to say something, but she couldn't find the words. She moved her hands to rest on her knees and she focused on her breathing.

Caiden kneeled in front of her and touched her face, and her forehead to check for fever.

"She. Responded."

For someone who didn't want to be overly dramatic, it seemed as though she was very dramatic. She watched Caiden read her aunt's email then he turned to her and smiled.

"That's fantastic."

She tried smiling but it felt off, tilted to one side and not what she meant it to be. "I'm so sorry. I'm taking this far differently than I ever dreamed."

Caiden gently wrapped his fingers around hers. "Baby, this is all natural. This is something that most people never go through in their lives and you can't just tell yourself how you'll act then do it. When your emotions take over, that's that. Ride the wave and then we'll talk."

She nodded her head vigorously and practiced her breathing. Caiden sat on the sofa and reread the email. Mia stood and paced the room a few times then came to sit next to Caiden. He handed her the laptop with a soft smile on his face.

"Thank you."

"Do you want me to leave while you write your email?"

"No. I'm simply going to respond and tell her yes, I'd love to video chat with her. Then she'll set up what she needs to set up."

Her fingers flew across the keys as she easily responded her few words. Then she closed the lid on her laptop and looked over at Caiden.

"I'm hungry."

She giggled. "I guess I am as well."

Mia stood and let out a deeply held breath clearing away all doubt and fear and took Caiden's proffered hand and happily joined him and his colleagues for dinner. As they made their way through the kitchen this time, she smiled at Sheldon as they walked through, and she spied his broad smile from the corner of her eye.

Dinner was placed on the buffet along the inside wall of the dining room; the opposite wall had windows looking out onto the yard area where she'd sat chatting with Shelby, Yvette, Isi, and Charly today.

They filled their plates with the aromatic meatloaf, mashed potatoes, and carrots Sheldon had created.

"Do you eat like this all the time?"

Charly laughed. "I can tell you Sam doesn't."

The others at the table laughed, including Sam, and Caiden explained, "Charly is trying to learn to cook."

Sam swallowed his food. "She's doing good."

Charly nudged him. "Because we come here a couple times a week or Sheldon is a god and sends meals home with me."

Emmy walked in, her brows furrowed and her face contorted in pain.

Mia watched her fill her plate. "Are you okay, Emmy?"

Emmy limped to the table and sat down carefully. "I have a messed-up hip from an IED explosion and, let's just say, some days are better than others."

"I'm so sorry."

Charly set her fork down and locked eyes with Mia. "We're all damaged in some way here Mia." She held up her left arm as proof. "That's why we're here. It doesn't mean we aren't beneficial, it means we work differently than most."

She shrugged and picked up her fork and scooped up some mashed potatoes. Mia glanced at Sam but he was staring at his wife and the look made her feel all warm and squishy inside. You could see their love.

Emmy took a drink of her tea and said, "Piper's coming home."

"What?" Charly exclaimed. "She never said a word, when is she coming home?"

Emmy smiled. "To be fair I just got off the phone with her. They'll be back here in two days. Royce is finished with football for the season and it sounds like he's trying to make a decision on whether or not to return. This was a shitty year for him and the Sinners. In light of all the things, the Sinners have agreed he can walk from his contract as long as he doesn't publicly say anything about the trafficking."

Mia sat back in her chair. "What about what he's already said?"

"Your articles are already out there Mia. It would be next to impossible to take them back. They've likely been saved on thousands of servers and hard drives."

Mia looked over at Caiden and he smiled. "Plus, there are ways around everything. If you look for them."

Charly laughed and Sam shook his head. "I don't want to hear anything else about skirting the law."

Charly looked at Mia. "Sam's a cop."

"Detective."

"Same thing."

She laughed and he wrapped his arm around her shoulders and pulled her over. "Take it back."

Their laughter filled the room.

45

Caiden walked into the conference room the following morning and found Emmy sitting at her desk.

"Caiden, I'm glad you're here."

He walked to her desk and sat at the end of the conference table facing her. "Okay. Should I be worried?"

Emmy laughed. "What do you know that I don't?"

Caiden sat forward. Now he was wondering if that was a loaded question or not. "I'll let you go first."

Emmy laughed. "Just busting your balls."

"Whew."

"How's Mia handling being here?"

"She's settling in. She likes everyone and everyone seems to like her. She's adjusting to being amid a lot of people, which she isn't used to, but she hasn't complained at all."

"Good." Emmy stopped moving papers on her desk and looked at him. "Will she be staying?"

"As in long-term?"

"As in long-term."

"We haven't talked about anything beyond the trial. But, I don't see anything changing unless she decides she wants a house outside of the compound."

Emmy smiled at him and nodded. "You look happy."

He relaxed his back, he'd been unsure of the direction of this conversation. "I am happy."

"So, let's keep it that way. I think you should make your plans to take Mia back to West Virginia right away. We're in a bit of a holding pattern right now."

"Holding pattern?"

"Dildo and Jasper have gone dark. Likely scared of the hacker. Deacon is working on the hacker's location and Piper's working on getting information from Bobby Lee. And Vegas police are looking for Spivey. Holding pattern."

"Okay. So I should take this time to get Mia sorted with her family. See where it all heads?"

"It's a good time don't you think? You can be reached by telephone, email, and text. Take your laptop and sort out your stuff. Piper will be home tomorrow and we'll be covered here."

He sat back and thought it all through. Mia's Aunt Rebecca had wanted to talk to her; they could simply meet in person. His parents would offer a neutral space for that and he'd get to see them again.

"It seems perfect. Thanks Emmy."

"Hey, when we started RAPTOR we all agreed it would be a place we all wanted to be. We'd get the job done, stop traffickers, and save as many lives as we could. But, most importantly, we look after each other. This is me looking after you. Take the plane."

His eyes watered. "Thanks Emmy. I apprec... We both appreciate it."

He stood and tried not to run to the door so he could tell Mia what was going on. As soon as he was in the elevator he yelped and fist pumped the air. He took long strides to reach their apartment on the first floor. When he opened the door he heard the shower and paced the living room waiting for her. Then, he thought, 'fuck it' and stripped his clothes off and joined her.

The warm water sliding down her sweet body made his cock thicken. When he stepped in with her and she turned in his arms, his lips sought hers. Mia slid her fingers down his torso and slowly let them find his cock, which she sweetly wrapped her fingers around and pumped.

He backed her up to the wall of the shower and slid his left arm under her right leg, lifting it off the ground.

Her eyes locked on his and her lips parted in a sassy smile. His heart was full and he was ready.

He bent his knees and Mia gently led his cock to her entrance. He pushed up into her and they both moaned. It wasn't easy this way, but it was hot.

She used her fingers on her clit and he pushed into her over and over again until his balls pulled up so tightly into his body he thought he'd scream in pain. Mia then called out his name as she climaxed, and he eagerly followed her to the end.

He let her leg slide down his as they gathered their breath. Her arms wrapped around his waist and her head lay against his chest. Caiden closed his eyes and enjoyed this feeling. This moment in time was one of so many more he hoped they'd have.

After showering Caiden walked into the bedroom to dress but decided to watch Mia dress first. "We're going to West Virginia."

Her eyes rounded. "When?"

"Emmy said to go right away and take the plane."

"Oh my God. I'm excited and nervous."

"I'll call my parents and see if they'll provide a neutral private place to meet your Aunt Rebecca, and the two of you can decide if and when to tell Ashton."

Mia launched herself at him and he fell back on the bed holding her in his arms.

She kissed his lips, her fingers slid into his hair and massaged his scalp and he absorbed it all.

"Thank you." She whispered against his lips.

"Thank *you.*"

She giggled. "For what?"

"For being here. For being alive. For being."

"Caid."

"Shall we get ready? We've got a lot of arrangements to make."

"Yeah."

He reluctantly helped her off him, then got dressed. He called his mom first. Then he called Therese. Mia emailed her Aunt Rebecca and they packed a light bag for each of them. Laptops over their shoulders and suitcases in hand, they exited the compound headed for a reunion, hopefully two, and the beginning of settling everything that needed to be settled.

46

Mia sat at the kitchen table in Caiden's parents' home and watched her Aunt Rebecca read the last of Mia's written accounting of what had happened to her.

Aunt Rebecca's fingers shook and Uncle David gently took the papers from his wife's hands when she finished and did his own study of them.

Caiden reached over and held her hand as they quietly waited for questions. Her stomach was in knots and the reception when they'd first laid eyes on each other was cool at best, but now her Aunt Rebecca jumped up from her chair and hugged Mia tightly.

"I was so afraid to believe it was true. That you were—are still alive."

"Thank you for all you've done over the years for Ashton. And I'm so sorry that I ran."

Aunt Rebecca shushed her. "Oh honey, I'm so sorry for all you've gone through. Wanda was my sister and I loved her so much. When your father left I wanted to go find him and kill him myself for leaving you two high and dry. Three actually, with Ashton."

Mia squeezed her aunt tightly and closed her eyes pretending for just a few minutes she was hugging her mom.

Aunt Rebecca pulled away and looked into her eyes. "You look just like her."

Mia sniffed and swiped at her tears. "I was going to say the same thing to you."

With the formality of the first meeting out of the way, Caiden's mom stood from the table and said, "Why don't we all go and sit in the living room where it's more comfortable?"

Roseanne fussed and fretted, making sure everyone had a full drink and plenty of pillows to lean against to be comfortable. Cole, Caiden's father, scolded his wife lovingly. "For crying out loud Roseanne, stop fussing."

Roseanne shushed him and fussed a bit more. Mia giggled a little, because they were funny and because she felt light and giddy after the oppression of the past hour and retelling her story and answering questions.

"Aunt Rebecca? How do you think Ashton will take seeing me again? What is his condition?"

"He had a head injury due to the car accident after you were gone. He's improved a bit over time and with therapy. He struggles with some of his speech. He can feed himself but it takes a long time. He still does therapy three times a week at the nursing home. He can take a few steps but it's exhausting for him, so he uses a wheelchair."

Mia listened and blinked rapidly to keep the tears from falling. She'd cried more in the past month than she had the last fifteen years. That first year she was on her own, she cried every night. Then, she stopped crying.

"Does he remember me?"

"He does, honey. He often tells me he misses you."

This time she did break down and cry. "I miss him too."

Caiden pulled her into his arms and kissed the top of her head. While Mia cried Caiden asked, "How do you propose we tell him Mia's alive and here?"

"I'll call the nursing home tonight when I get home and find out what his therapist thinks is best. But I suspect we'll just bring Mia to see him and see if he recognizes her."

Roseanne pulled some tissues from a box on the side table and handed them to Mia. "Thank you," she whispered then dried her eyes.

She sat up straighter but held Caiden's hand as she looked at her Aunt Rebecca fight back tears herself.

Mia smiled at her. "Can you tell me about the boys? How are they?"

Mia's cousins, Adam and Austin were close to seven years younger than she was.

Rebecca looked at David while she wiped her tears and he nodded.

"Adam is twenty-six now and he works over in St. George's Ridge as an accountant. Austin is twenty-four and just finished up his master's degree in chemical engineering. He's looking at jobs now. They are going to be excited to see you again Mia."

"I'm excited to see them again too."

David then looked at Caiden, "Tell us what you do Caiden. Your parents are always so secretive about everything."

Caiden chuckled and looked at his parents. "I work for an agency that exists solely to end the trafficking of women and children. I'm a special operative and work in the cyber unit. Beyond saying that, we fly under the radar generally and keep a low profile."

David and Rebecca both stared at Caiden with their mouths hanging open. Mia laughed at the look on their faces. "You should meet the whole team. They're fierce."

Caiden smiled at her and then leaned down and kissed her lips. It made her feel so good. It was a subtle way to let everyone know they were together, though he'd been by her side for the past few weeks, this was a statement on its own.

"I hope we get to meet them one day."

Mia smiled at her uncle. "I do too; you won't forget a single one of them."

Rebecca stood. "I'm going to call Ashton's therapist now and see if we can see him tomorrow."

She stepped out on the front porch and Mia squeezed Caiden's hand. "It'll be okay, baby."

"I sure hope so."

47

They walked into the nursing home side by side. Mia's hand squeezed his so tightly that if he were a lesser man he'd have squealed. Rebecca was a few steps ahead of them and the nursing staff on duty stared as they walked past them to Ashton's room.

"Ms. Stewart?" One of the nurses called out.

Mia hesitated then turned. "Me?"

The older lady came to stand in front of Mia. "I wanted to thank you for coming to give evidence against Dominick Nelson. He ruined my daughter's life many years ago. She turned to drugs and she's been in and out of rehab over the past few years. She can't kick the habit and it's all because of him."

Mia's lip quivered as she stared into this woman's weary eyes. "I'm so sorry."

"I just wanted you to know that I appreciate you getting that son of a bitch off the streets."

Mia swallowed and then reached out and hugged the woman. Caiden's throat convulsed as he swallowed watching these two share in silent support of each other.

Her Aunt Rebecca had stopped and watched, and her eyes were glistening too.

The woman stepped back and sniffed. "I'll let you go see your brother. He's going to be so excited to see you."

"I hope so."

Mia turned and took his hand again and they continued down the hall to Ashton's room. The home was decorated nicely and not at all a utilitarian feel to it. Flowers in vases were placed on small tables before each doorway. The carpeting was a nice tan color with small specks of burgundy and orange in it. Finally Rebecca stopped at a door, and a table on the right side of the door said, Ashton Stewart.

Rebecca looked at Mia first then him, "Ready?"

"Yes." Mia nodded. She squeezed his hand tighter. He'd have to remember to tell her she had a monstrous grip.

Rebecca opened the door and stepped inside, and he could hear Ashton say in slurred speech. "Where is she?"

He pulled his hand from hers and ushered her into the room, but he was close behind her.

"Mia!" Ashton yelled.

Mia ran to him and kneeled in front of his chair and wrapped her arms around him. He hugged her close and cried into her hair. Caiden stood and watched them. He wanted to remember this day forever. It was simply beautiful.

"I missed Mia."

"I missed you too, Ash."

Rebecca introduced him to Ashton's therapist. "This is Connie. She's been Ashton's therapist for eight or so years now."

Caiden shook her hand. "It's nice to meet you, Connie."

"Same here."

Connie quietly told him much of what Rebecca had told them yesterday. She'd mentioned to Ashton a few minutes before they arrived that Mia was alive and she was here to see him. If he would have reacted badly they would have called and told them not to come. Connie then whispered, "He's been lonely. His whole family was gone."

Caiden nodded. He didn't know but could only imagine how that would feel to him.

They stayed at the nursing home for two hours until Ashton grew tired.

"Promise you come back, Mia." He'd said when Connie told him he needed to rest.

"I promise Ash. How about tomorrow?"

"Yay!"

A few more hugs, tears, and goodbyes and he took Mia's hand, which gratefully wasn't as strong on the way out. Rebecca hugged them both in the parking lot. "Please join us for dinner tonight. The boys will be coming home to see you. Caiden, bring your parents, please. We all are so pleased to have more family to embrace."

"I'll ask them. Thank you."

"Aunt Rebecca, can we bring something?"

"No, honey. Just come and join us."

"We will." Mia looked up at him with questioning eyes. "Yes, of course."

He opened the driver's door of Rebecca's car as she climbed in, then he wrapped his arm around Mia and walked with her to their rented car.

Mia chattered all the way back to his parents. The final burden of meeting and telling family what had happened finally lifted from her shoulders.

When they got back to his parents' house, Mia needed a nap and he settled her into his old room, then stepped out to spend some time with his parents.

"How did it go?"

"It went well. He was thrilled to see her. Lots of tears. Lots of hugs."

"I'm so happy to hear that."

His father, not so subtle, "So?"

"So?"

"Are you getting married?"

Caiden stared at his father, never one to bullshit and nodded. "I hope so. I've been debating when the best time to ask her is. She's had a lot on her plate these past few weeks and I don't want her to agree to marry me out of a sense of duty. I don't want her to regret saying yes. I don't want to put more on her plate if she has a lot to think about. Things have been changing so fast that I want her to know what she wants when I ask her."

"I do."

He turned to see Mia standing in the kitchen doorway, her eyes locked on his.

He sat frozen. "I know what I want. I want you."

His mother gasped and he stood, slowly making his way to her. "I want you to be sure."

"I am."

"It's forever."

"I know."

"You've been through a lot."

"So have you. Do you know what you want?"

He looked deeply into her eyes. The chocolate brown he'd fallen in love with seventeen years ago. "I want you."

She smiled but her eyes never left his.

"Will you marry me?"

"Yes."

EPILOGUE

His mom and Rebecca pranced around them, fussing and fluttering, and he was ready to take Mia and run away.

His mom pinned a boutonnière onto his suit jacket. "I've never in my life pulled a wedding together this fast. I think I could start a business and call it "Quickies".

"Mom, that has a different connotation to it than weddings."

"Really?" She gasped, then muttered, "Oh, yes, that won't do."

"Roseanne, will you stop fussing? You're making me nervous."

"Our son isn't getting married ever again and there was no time. I just want it to be perfect."

"It's not about the wedding it's about the marriage."

"I know that. Boy, you're cranky today."

His dad laughed and winked in his direction and Caiden couldn't help it, he laughed too. Mia stood across the room, a robe covering her dress, with Rebecca fussing over her hair and her earrings. "These are something old. Your mother gave them to me for my twentieth birthday. God bless her soul. She'd be so proud of you Mia." She pulled out a necklace with a thin gold chain and a small diamond at the center. "This is something new; it's from David and me."

Caiden's mom ran across the room with a silk clutch purse. "This is something borrowed. It was mine when I married that old crab across the room."

Mia grinned and looked into his eyes. He laughed. His parents were a hoot. Caiden had a blue kerchief in his pocket. He pulled it out, "This is something blue. I wore it when Cord married Deborah, so it's also borrowed, but mostly it's blue."

He handed it to her and leaned in to kiss her, but his mother yelled, "Oh no you don't. You aren't married yet."

"Mom, you've seen me kiss Mia before."

"That was then, this is now."

He looked at Mia and shrugged, and she winked.

"Now go on with you. Scoot on out and make sure everyone is here."

"Adam and Austin are the ushers."

"Just go on now."

He walked past his dad, "Come on, Dad, or you'll get scolded too."

"Jeezzuz, it's so a man can't sit in his own house anymore."

He walked outside and looked around the yard. Chairs had been borrowed from the church and set up in the yard. Flowers graced the altar brought from the church at the front where he'd become Mia's husband. Family, neighbors, friends from all over had come to join them. No one from RAPTOR was able to make it as chatter had started up again, but he promised to have the ceremony recorded and share it with them. He and Mia had to fly back tonight so he could resume his mission, and she was such a trooper she happily agreed.

The minister walked up to him. "Are you ready, Caiden?"

"I am. Are you ready?"

The minister laughed. "I've done this thousands of times. Hopefully this will be your only time."

"Yes sir. I agree."

He nodded and called through the door of the house.

"Mom, you wanna send my bride out, it's time to get us married."

He heard giggles and chattering and smiled as he walked to the front of the chairs by the altar.

Mia's Uncle David pulled up in a car and walked around to the passenger side and helped Ashton out of the car. He situated himself in his wheelchair and David pushed him up by Caiden. Caiden bent down and shook his hand. "Thank you for doing me the honor, Ashton."

Ashton smiled. "You be good to her."

"Yes sir, I sure will."

Ashton nodded and the music started.

He looked up to see Mia's Aunt Rebecca walking down the aisle toward him. Her smile was bright and happy. Mia had said that Rebecca looked just like her mother and Mia said the same about Rebecca, so he imagined that's what Mia would look like in about twenty years, and he wasn't disappointed. The music grew louder and Mia appeared at the end of the chairs, regal and elegant in a gorgeous white gown. He'd heard his mom fussing over a dress the past couple of days and he imagined she either altered it or made it; he'd find out later. Whatever it had been, she'd done a beautiful job.

Mia floated down the aisle and stood beside him. "You look beautiful."

"You're handsome as ever, Caiden."

Mia's Uncle David walked to Ashton and helped him stand. "I stand for this." Ashton beamed.

Mia smiled at him, stepped up to him and gave him a kiss on the cheek.

The minister said some nice things, they repeated their vows and he placed a gold band on her finger with a vow that they'd go shopping and buy her real rings when they got back to Lynyrd Station. For now, this was his grandmother's ring.

He slid it on her finger and said, "Forever and always."

Mia smiled, "Forever and always."

As soon as the minister said, "You may kiss your bride," Caiden turned and looked at his mother, his eyebrows up in his hairline.

"Now you can kiss her, dear."

Everyone got a good laugh and Caiden kissed his bride.

They enjoyed a few drinks and toasts; the ladies from church brought the best food a person could ask for. Honestly, there was nothing better than a church potluck. And at eight o'clock, they had to say their goodbyes.

He'd called a car to take them to the airport, since he'd enjoyed a few drinks. They climbed in just as his phone buzzed.

"Marx."

"It's Emmy. Congratulations."

"Thank you. How are things going?"

"Things are heating up. Deacon thinks he's pinpointed the hacker's location, he's trying to confirm now. And Jasper is chattering again."

"We're headed to the airport now. Should be home in a couple of hours."

"I'm sorry, Caiden. I promise you'll get time to take a honeymoon."

"I want to be in on this as much as everyone else. We'll get our honeymoon."

"Thank you. We're getting close."

He turned to Mia and shrugged. "Duty calls."

Mia smiled at him, "Then we'd better get going. I don't want you to miss getting those bastards."

He kissed her softly, "I love you Mia. Thank you for understanding."

She giggled, "I love you too, but honestly, I'm as invested in stopping these assholes as you are."

His phone buzzed and he looked at the screen. A text from Deacon, "Our hacker is butting into our chatter channel once again. It looks as though our hacker is a young girl named Becca Bentley. We're narrowing down a location."

* Deacon is about to meet hacker Becca. How do you think that will play out? Find out in Believing Becca, RAPTOR Book Six.

ALSO BY PJ FIALA

Click here to see a list of all of my books with the blurbs.

Contemporary Romance

Rolling Thunder Series

Moving to Love, Book 1

Moving to Hope, Book 2

Moving to Forever, Book 3

Moving to Desire, Book 4

Moving to You, Book 5

Moving Home, Book 6

Moving On, Book 7

Rolling Thunder Boxset, Books 1-3

Military Romantic Suspense

Second Chances Series

Designing Samantha's Love, Book 1

Securing Kiera's Love, Book 2

Second Chances Boxset - Duet

Bluegrass Security Series

Heart Thief, Book One

Finish Line, Book Two

Lethal Love, Book Three

Wrenched Fate, Book Four

Bluegrass Security Boxset, Books 1-3

Big 3 Security

Ford: Finding His Fire Book One

Lincoln: Finding His Mark Book Two

Dodge: Finding His Jewel Book Three

Rory: Finding His Match Book Four

Big 3 Security Boxset, Books 1-3

GHOST

Defending Keirnan, GHOST Book One

Defending Sophie, GHOST Book Two

Defending Roxanne, GHOST Book Three

Defending Yvette, GHOST Book Four

Defending Bridget, GHOST Book Five

Defending Isabella, GHOST Book Six

RAPTOR

RAPTOR Rising - Prequel

Saving Shelby, RAPTOR Book One

Holding Hadleigh, RAPTOR Book Two

Craving Charlesia, RAPTOR Book Three

Promising Piper, RAPTOR Book Four

Missing Mia, RAPTOR Book Five

Believing Becca, RAPTOR Book Six

Keeping Kori, RAPTOR Book Seven

Healing Hope, RAPTOR Book Eight

Engaging Emersyn, RAPTOR Book Nine

ENJOY THIS BOOK? YOU CAN MAKE A BIG DIFFERENCE

Reviews are the most powerful tools in my arsenal when it comes to getting attention for my books. As much as I'd like to, I don't have the financial muscle of a New York publisher. I can't take out full page ads in the newspaper or put posters on the subway.

(Not yet, anyway.)

But I do have something much more powerful and effective than that, and it's something that those big publishers would die to get their hands on.

A committed and loyal bunch of readers.

Honest reviews of my books help bring them to the attention of other readers.

If you've enjoyed this book I would be so grateful to you if you could spend just five minutes leaving a review (it can be as short as you like) on the book's vendor page. You can jump right to the page of your choice by clicking the link below.

Thank you so very much.

MEET PJ

Writing has been a desire my whole life. Once I found the courage to write, life changed for me in the most profound way. Bringing stories to readers that I'd enjoy reading and creating characters that are flawed, but lovable is such a joy.

When not writing, I'm with my family doing something fun. My husband, Gene, and I are bikers and enjoy riding to new locations, meeting new people and generally enjoying this fabulous country we live in.

I come from a family of veterans. My grandfather, father, brother, two sons, and one daughter-in-law are all veterans. Needless to say, I am proud to be an American and proud of the service my amazing family has given.

My online home is https://www.pjfiala.com.
You can connect with me on Facebook at https://www.facebook.com/PJFiala1,
and
Instagram at https://www.Instagram.com/PJFiala.
If you prefer to email, go ahead, I'll respond - pjfiala@pjfiala.com.

Made in the USA
Monee, IL
23 September 2022